Sleeping With The Enemy

Lisa Dyble

Copyright © 2012 by Lisa Dyble.

Library of Congress Control Number:		2012917602
ISBN:	Hardcover	978-1-4797-2104-7
	Softcover	978-1-4797-2103-0
	Ebook	978-1-4797-2105-4

All rights reserved. No part of this book may be reproduced or transmitted in any form or by any means, electronic or mechanical, including photocopying, recording, or by any information storage and retrieval system, without permission in writing from the copyright owner.

This is a work of fiction. Names, characters, places and incidents either are the product of the author's imagination or are used fictitiously, and any resemblance to any actual persons, living or dead, events, or locales is entirely coincidental.

This book was printed in the United States of America.

To order additional copies of this book, contact:
Xlibris Corporation
1-888-795-4274
www.Xlibris.com
Orders@Xlibris.com
120549

Chapter One

A thin whisper of moonlight escaped into the room from around the edge of the window blind, its faint glow only just outlining the few simple furnishings within. The man stepped slowly but deliberately across the floor toward the sleeping woman, grim determination evident in every inch of his stiff, unyielding profile. The linoleum creaked under his weight, and he froze midstep, listening carefully. Satisfied by the even rhythm of her breathing, he again moved forward.

He stopped at the foot of the bed and glanced down at its occupant, reluctantly admiring the way the long golden curls strewn across the pillow so beautifully framed her petite features. A slight frown creased his brow as he noted the large bandage taped across her forehead. It made her look so helpless, so vulnerable and alone.

Impatient with his thoughts, he deliberately looked away, focusing instead on the hospital chart hanging off the metal bed frame. He removed the clipboard from its hook and squinted down at the tiny print, but was unable to read a word of it. One hand reached down into his pocket to grab his keys. Holding them immobile in his fist, he shone a thin beam of light onto the paper from a tiny penlight attached to the key ring.

Aside from the gash to her forehead, she appeared to be unhurt, save for minor cuts and bruises. The woman was lucky; the bushes must have broken her fall. Satisfied by what he'd read, he shoved the key ring back into his pocket and returned the clipboard to its resting spot, still careful not to make a sound. He then moved around to the far side of the bed.

Wade Scott rubbed his chin absently as he once again examined the sleeping beauty, dimly noting somewhere in the back of his mind that he was badly in need of a shave. His eyes narrowed as he noted her sudden restless movements, and he wondered what she was dreaming about. Perhaps it had something to do with whatever had gotten his brother-in-law killed.

The door handle clicked unexpectedly, and he instinctively dropped to the floor, using the bed for cover. His lips shaped a silent curse, for he had no desire to be caught in here. Visiting hours were long over, and besides, he'd already been told that visitors wouldn't be permitted until at least the following day. A run-in with hospital security was not a concept he particularly relished, given that he wasn't on very good terms with cops in general these days.

The door clicked shut, and Wade instinctively held his breath as he heard footsteps move across the room toward the bed. Perhaps if he were lucky, the nurse would simply take the woman's temperature or whatever else it was that she had to do and then get on about her business elsewhere. He waited, hardly daring to breathe, lest he give himself away.

There was a faint rustle of clothing, accompanied by a sharp exhalation of breath that echoed harshly in the still silence of the room. The person on the opposite side of the bed was breathing in short, shallow gasps, as if he or she were nervous. A warning prickled at the back of Wade's neck.

He heard a brief scraping sound, and moments later, a strange odor assailed his nostrils, sharply pungent with just a hint of sweetness.

Wade leaped to his feet with a snarl, now convinced the unexpected visitor wasn't part of the medical staff. Before the astonished stranger could react, Wade's left hand snaked across the bed and knocked the jar from his hand. The glass bottle hit the floor and shattered, sending fragments of glass and droplets of chloroform scattering across the room.

The would-be assailant followed close behind, momentarily stunned from the hard right to the side of his jaw which knocked him two steps backward and onto his rear. Cursing, the man scrambled to his feet and stumbled toward the door. Wade leaped into action, but by the time he'd made his way around the bed, the other man had already wrenched open the door and disappeared out into the hallway.

Wade followed in hot pursuit, but as he raced across the room, he slipped on the chloroform. Thrown off balance, he almost went down, and by the time he'd recovered, the hallway was empty. Down at the far end of the hall, the door to the stairs swung back into place with a gentle swish, signaling the direction of the assailant's hasty retreat.

Giving up the chase, he turned his attention back to the woman. The chloroform-soaked rag was still covering her nose and mouth. Knocking the cloth aside, he grabbed her shoulder and shook it lightly, to no avail. He nudged her a little harder, but there was still no response. The chloroform had done its job only too well; she was dead to the world.

He swore aloud, smashing one fist into opposite palm in frustration. What a mess. She would be out cold for some time, and he couldn't stay much longer; the risk of getting caught was increasing with each passing moment. But he wasn't about to leave her alone in the room with the mystery assailant still on the loose. For all Wade knew, the man could very well be the one responsible for Cliff's death.

When evidence of the attempted assault was discovered, the police would no doubt put her under twenty-four-hour guard. Once that happened, he would be completely cut off from her, for there was no way she would willingly speak with him. And if the cops somehow managed to link her to Cliff, they might even accuse *him* of attacking her with the chloroform. After all, he had been the one to call 911 for help earlier that afternoon when he'd seen her fall from her apartment balcony. The police might well find his presence first at that mishap and then at this one a little too coincidental for their liking. Especially once Tanya awoke and told them how much she hated his guts.

With a sigh of resignation, he reached down and scooped her up into his arms, blanket and all, knowing full well this was a decision he was going to regret. But right now, he needed answers, even if he had to beat them out of her.

His gaze softened involuntarily as he glanced down at the still figure in his arms. The poor girl had taken quite a beating this afternoon already without him adding to her pain and misery. But if he didn't get her out of here, who knew what might happen to her? After this unexpected turn of events, he was quite certain her fall had been no accident.

Opening the door as quietly as possible, he peeked out into the hallway, first one direction, then the other. The recent staff cutbacks were working in his favor; there was no one in sight. He took a deep breath. It was now or never.

Wade dashed down the hall toward the direction of the elevators. An empty wheelchair sitting just outside the now-deserted patient lounge caught his eye, and he paused long enough to settle his burden inside it, tucking the blanket solicitously around her bruised and battered body in a somewhat belated attempt to salve his burning conscience. Hopefully from a distance, the white jacket he had "borrowed" earlier would allow him to pass for one of the medical staff should anyone happen to notice them.

The elevator began its silent descent. Wade watched the numbers on the panel light up as they continued past each floor, silently praying that no one would interrupt their journey. After what seemed an eternity, the elevator glided to a gentle stop at level 2 of the underground parking.

Wade tensed as the doors opened and then relaxed at the empty silence which greeted him. Moving quickly, he wheeled the girl over to the parking payment machine and inserted first his parking stub and then his credit card. He tapped his foot impatiently as the transaction took what seemed an eternity to process. Finally, his receipt spit out, and he shoved both it and the credit card into his jacket pocket.

Scooping the woman into his arms, Wade threw caution to the wind and raced toward his truck which was now sitting out in the open a hundred yards away. Moving quickly, he settled his comatose passenger into the back bench of the crew cab and laid the blanket down over top of her. He then stuffed the white jacket underneath the front seat. All was quiet as he reached the exit and inserted his parking ticket into the machine. The security arm lifted, and he breathed a heartfelt sigh of relief as he exited the parking garage without issue.

Wade pulled out into the street, flexing his fingers in an effort to steady his shaking hands as the full import of what he had just done struck home with sudden, brutal clarity. Kidnapping was a serious offense, and if he didn't do some fast talking when Tanya woke up, he would be doing some hard time in the slammer for his crime, a fitting punishment that would no doubt bring her a great deal of pleasure.

He drove to a practically deserted Motel 6 just off the I-405 and managed to sneak her inside without being seen. After tucking her into the bed, he poured himself a stiff whiskey and settled back to wait for her return to consciousness. He was unclear as to how long this might take, but one thing he did know for sure. From what he remembered of Tanya Riverton, she was going to be mad as hell at him when she woke up. It made no difference that he had probably saved her life; he knew from experience that she was the most unreasonable woman he'd ever met.

Chapter Two

Sunlight streaming through the thin curtains gently teased the woman's eyes open. The first thing she saw was a huge bear of a man with fur all over his face stretched out in a chair across the room from her. His denim-clad legs seemed to go on forever before crossing at the ankles to reveal two stockinged feet, one with a small hole worn through at the heel. A pair of black work boots lay a short distance away where he had obviously kicked them off sometime earlier. A long sleeved T-shirt hugged his upper body, not quite camouflaging the bulge of muscle across his chest. His arms looked like tree trunks; his hands large and powerful. Beneath the stubble on his face was the outline of a hard, square jaw. She sensed in him a powerful ally. Or a formidable foe.

Glancing past the man, she studied her surroundings with growing confusion. The room was unfamiliar, and with a start, she realized she had no idea where she was or how she had got there. It was a safe bet to assume the man in the chair had brought her, but for what purpose? She had absolutely no idea who he was or, for that matter, whether he was friend or foe. Panic tightened in her gut, sending her heart into a flurry of palpitations, but she bit back the momentary fear with cool determination. No one, not even that lumberjack of a man, was going to push her around. She wanted some answers, and she was going to get them now.

"Hey, mister," she called out. Her voice came out as a weak croak, and she wondered if he'd heard her. A moment later, the man opened his eyes and shifted his huge bulk in the chair, which suddenly seemed two sizes too small for him.

"What am I doing here . . . and who the hell are you?"

Wade blinked himself awake, aware the moment of truth was upon him. This was indeed the Tanya he remembered; the challenge in her tone hadn't changed one bit. He ignored the second question for the time being, choosing instead to answer the first.

"You were attacked at the hospital, so I brought you here for safety."

"What was I doing in the hospital?" she asked hesitantly, her mind a disconcerting total blank on the subject.

"You mean you don't remember?"

She realized that indeed she did not. She tried to shift her brain into gear, but it hurt to think. A shaft of pain knifed through her skull, and she lifted her hand to her head in automatic reflex. Her fingers touched the bandage taped to her forehead, and she winced in pain. The skin was swollen and tender beneath the dressing.

"What happened to my head?"

"You don't remember?" he repeated, starting to feel a little confused himself. Perhaps the blow to her head had affected her immediate short-term memory.

"Is there an echo in here?" she demanded irritably.

He ground his teeth and prayed for patience. The damn woman had the most annoying ability to get on his nerves simply by opening her mouth.

"You fell from your apartment balcony yesterday afternoon and injured your head," he explained, pointedly ignoring her smart remark. "Someone came at you with a bottle of chloroform at the hospital last night, so in order to ensure your safety, I brought you here."

She was silent for almost a minute, digesting his remarks.

"How do I know you're telling me the truth?" she started up again, a renewed challenge in her tone. "Maybe you're the one who chloroformed me. How do I know you didn't push me off the balcony? How do I know you're not the guy who wants me dead?"

"For Chrissakes, lady," he interrupted irritably, rising to his feet to place his hands on his hips and stare down at her in exasperation. "You're still alive, aren't you?"

She stared up at him, unable to think of a suitably sharp rejoinder. In fact, all her mind could focus on at the moment was the menacing way he towered over her. He was so big his back blocked the light from the window. In the absence of the sun's rays, the temperature in the room seemed suddenly cooler, and she shivered involuntarily.

Perhaps she would think better on her feet. Favoring him with a baleful glare, she tossed the covers back from her body and swung her legs around the side of the bad, wincing again as she did so. Her mind may not be aware of what had happened to her, but her body certainly remembered what it had been through. She hurt everywhere.

Her eyes widened as she realized she was dressed in nothing but a skimpy hospital gown, the kind that left her backside wide open to the breeze. She snatched at the hospital blanket lying loose on top of the bed and wrapped it around her body, throwing a silent, accusatory stare at the man in front of her. His responding look of derision made her feel a little foolish.

"I need a hot shower," she grumbled, rising to her feet.

He noted the pain etched across her face, and both his temper and his manner softened somewhat. "A hot bath would be better," he suggested.

"I hate baths," she sniffed in disdain.

"Suit yourself, Tanya," he shrugged indifferently and stepped back out of her way, knowing full well she was going to do just that.

She paused a moment in the doorway to the bathroom, her face screwed up in confusion. "Is that my name?"

"You really don't remember?"

His only answer was the slamming of the bathroom door.

Wade scratched at his beard thoughtfully, reminding himself once again that he really should shave soon. Amnesia? It opened up some interesting possibilities.

A thoughtful smile curved his lips as he considered for a moment the sorely tempting opportunity to exact retribution, a long overdue payback for all the trouble she had delighted in causing him over the years. Perhaps it was high time the nasty bitch got some of her own back. Maybe this was the Lord's mysterious way of rewarding him for his saintly patience in dealing with her. A full-fledged grin of devilish delight lit up his features at the thought.

But no, he could never live with himself if he gave into temptation and took advantage of her vulnerability. He sighed heavily, acknowledging to himself that as soon as she had finished showering, he was going to have to 'fess up and tell her who he was. At least her injured body might slow her down long enough for him to escape the worst of the teeth and claws she would no doubt unsheathe upon discovering herself alone in the same room with Wade Scott, the man she was determined to destroy.

On the other hand, coming clean wouldn't get him any closer to finding out who had murdered his brother-in-law, for he was definitely the last person on earth Tanya would consider sharing any knowledge of the situation with. And he desperately needed to know what she did about the situation, for the safety of his sister and the sake of his two nephews.

Given similar circumstances, Tanya wouldn't hesitate an instant in using him to get what she wanted. So why should it be any different for him?

He put his head in his hand and groaned aloud, wishing the half-empty mickey of scotch on the edge of the dresser was still sitting unopened behind the backseat of his truck. It was hard to think straight when his head was pounding. He remembered the bottle of aspirin in the glove compartment of the truck and glanced around for his jacket. Spying it draped across the back of the chair he'd slept in, he reached inside the right pocket for his keys.

Tanya leaned against the shower stall and let the soothing heat soak its way into her aching bones as she examined the various cuts and bruises on her arms and legs. A dark discoloration was starting beneath the skin along one side of her ribs, making them sore to the touch. What on earth had her poor body been through?

And what was she doing alone in a seedy motel room with an antagonistic stranger, dressed only in a brief hospital gown with no back to it? Her face flamed as she realized he must have seen a full view of her rear end while transporting her here from the hospital.

The hot water continued to stream down over her body, removing bits of dirt and dried blood from her skin, but it was unable to wash away the cobwebs from her brain.

Who was she, and who was the person in the next room? What was her relationship to him? The man seemed vaguely familiar, but a stranger nonetheless. The more she searched for answers, the more questions she found.

What on earth was she going to do? What options did she have? Was the stranger in the next room planning on taking her somewhere? If she refused to go with him, where else could she go? Was there someone she could call to help her? And if she did call and someone came, would she know them, and more importantly, could she trust them? Questions, questions, and more questions. As each one rolled through her head she struggled to keep her growing panic at bay, aware that her very survival might well depend on her ability to stay calm and keep a clear head. No matter how frightening her present situation, she must do everything possible to keep her wits about her. Perhaps this apparent amnesia was only a temporary confusion, and all she needed to do was relax a little so that her memory could return.

That had to be the key to unlocking the door to her brain and putting the pieces of her mind back in order. It seemed, then, the best plan she had was to go with the flow until she figured out where it was leading her. That meant remaining calm, composed, and alert for clues as to who her captor was and what he wanted with her. The last thing she should do was give him the slightest inkling of how frightened she really was.

A spurt of anger erupted. How dare he frighten her like this? She had half a mind to march out into the next room right now and give him a piece of her mind. And start demanding some answers to some pretty basic questions while she was at it. After all, sometimes a best defense was a good offense.

A banging on the door interrupted her thoughts. "Are you okay in there?"

"I'm fine. Go away," she shouted back, only now just realizing how long she'd been in the shower. Her fingers were a mass of puffy wrinkles, and the skin around her toes was starting to look rather waterlogged. It was indeed time to shut the water off. She would have liked to wash her hair, but the bandage across her forehead made such a feat rather difficult. The soaping she'd given the ends would have to do.

Towelling off, she discovered she had yet a new problem to contend with. What was she going to wear? Her choices were limited to a green gown or a white towel, and neither did much to cover her body. A combination of the two would no doubt be her safest bet.

She used the hand towel to wipe the steam from the surface of the mirror and paused to examine her reflection. A complete stranger stared back at her. The long blonde tresses, the baby blue eyes, the pert little nose, and the generous lips could have belonged to someone else for all they meant to her. It was a most disconcerting feeling.

The banging on the door started again.

"Hurry up in there, will you?"

"Okay, okay already. Hold your horses, mister. I'm coming."

The door was barely open before he came barrelling inside and shoved her back into the main room in a none-too-gentlemanly fashion.

"About time," he muttered, just as he shut the door behind him.

The sound of nature calling from the bathroom caused her to experience a tiny twinge of guilt. The man had obviously been uncomfortable for a while.

Tanya sat down on the edge of the bed, her momentary feeling of bravado quickly fading as she wondered what to do next. She needed answers to some pretty basic questions, but right now her only source was of questionable reliability. His reason for being here with her remained a mystery, for she still had no idea who he was. She didn't even know his name. She sensed she had nothing to fear, but how could she trust her instincts when the rest of her senses were so fuzzy?

The sheer size of him was intimidating; he dwarfed the room just by being in it, and she felt like a midget next to him. She hadn't exactly been polite to him either. But could she help it if her head hurt?

The bathroom door opened, and the subject of her thoughts rushed through, a look of concern on his face as his eyes darted quickly around the room. His gaze fell upon her, and a look of relief crossed his features.

"You're still here," he stated unnecessarily.

She glanced down at her attire and then back up at him. "Where did you think I'd run off to?" she asked, her tone laced with sweet acidity.

"Hmph," he grunted. "Still your pleasant self, I see."

"Oh, really?" she retorted, her voice laced with disdain. "Well, I can't say you're being very pleasant either."

"Look," he began, "let's be reasonable about this."

"Speak for yourself," she cut in, her eyes snapping. "There's nothing wrong with *my* reasoning ability."

The hard set of his jaw gave her pause, and she experienced a faint twinge of apprehension. So far, this bear of a man had showed no sign of wanting to hurt her, but maybe, just maybe, she was beginning to push her luck.

"Okay," she continued in a more reasonable tone. "Are we related? I was just wondering how we came to be alone together in such unusual circumstances," she added hastily, in response to his raised eyebrow. She indicated their surroundings with a sweep of her open palm, eyes widening in sudden concern. "They are unusual, aren't they?" she added hesitantly.

Her earnest expression forced a reluctant smile to his lips. "Yes, they are unusual, and no, we aren't related."

"Then . . . do we know each other well? I mean, are we close? Oh, you know very well what I mean," she snapped as his smile evolved into a full-fledged grin of wicked amusement.

"Yes, we're close," he lied smoothly, having decided to string her along a bit until he received the answers he was looking for. Though not very honorable, it was nonetheless necessary. And if the truth be known, he felt very little guilt over it, for had she not brought this necessity on herself by being such a bitch toward him in the past?

"How close?"

He blinked, her directness disconcerting him.

"Close enough," he prevaricated, praying she would let it drop, and knowing full well that was like asking grass to grow purple.

"Then how come you slept on the chair all night, instead of in bed with me?"

"I was keeping a watch out for your attacker. I wasn't sure if he followed us here or not."

"With your eyes closed? Sorry, forget I said that. Couldn't resist." She grinned, holding up both hands to appease the thunderstorm brewing in his expression. "I know, I know. You fell asleep by accident, right? So why is someone after me? And forgive me for asking, but what's your name, by the way?"

"Wade Scott," he answered, watching her face carefully.

"Wade Scott," she repeated thoughtfully. Wade felt his body tense, and then relax when she added, "Sorry, that name doesn't mean a thing to me."

"I'm sure it will all come back very soon. Excuse me a moment, would you?"

Wanting answers and not about to wait for them, she followed him back into the bathroom and watched as he removed a bottle of aspirin from the front pocket of his jeans and knocked a double dosage into his hand. He then filled the water glass by the sink and downed it along with the pills in one huge swallow. She glanced through the bathroom doorway at the bottle of scotch on the edge of the dresser next to the chair he had slept in, comprehension dawning. He followed her gaze and grinned sheepishly as she turned back to him, a knowing look on her face.

"Serves me right," he muttered as he rinsed the glass and refilled it. "These might help your head a bit. How's the rest of you doing?" he asked sympathetically, offering her the glass along with the remaining aspirin.

She pulled a wry face. "I feel as if I've been run over by a Mac truck. Thanks," she added with a small but sincere smile as she accepted the peace offering. "I guess we could both use a little help this morning."

Wade stared down at her, lost in twin spheres of shimmering blue. Devoid of their usual hard glitter of angry accusation, they were the most beautiful eyes he had ever seen, as warm and inviting as a clear, summer sky, and filled with just as much promise of pleasure. Something tightened in his gut, and it was suddenly difficult to swallow. Now that for the first time in years they were no longer at odds with each other, he was finding Tanya Riverton extremely attractive. *This shouldn't be happening*, he reminded himself as one hand lifted of its own accord to caress her cheek.

Her skin was baby soft, except for the tiny scratch just below her eye. He touched it gently, sorely tempted to kiss the hurt away and make it better for her. Her softly quivering mouth was even more inviting, and he could no more fight the urge to kiss her than a moth could resist the seductive flickering of a candle's flame. A man could get seriously burned around a woman the likes of her.

Tanya stood transfixed by his silent scrutiny, conscious that her body was beginning to heat up under the intensity of his riveting gaze. Awareness became desire in the space of single heartbeat, and then all her previous confusion was replaced by the certain knowledge that she wanted desperately to touch her lips to his, to taste the delicious pleasures his gentle smile was hinting at. A small part of her mind dimly registered that she must be insane. Only a short while ago, she was accusing him of trying to overcome her with chloroform and push her out of her apartment balcony. Now, whoever he was, the stranger named Wade was going to kiss her, and it was more than fine by her.

A furious pounding on the door interrupted them just as their lips were about to make contact. They jumped apart, startled.

"Police! Open up Scott, we know you're in there."

Wade froze in alarm. "Damn." He must have been spotted at the hospital last night, after all.

"Wait a minute. What's wrong with the police being here?"

"I don't get along with cops very well these days," he told her grimly. "There's been a little misunderstanding between us." He sighed heavily and set her gently aside. "Time to face the music."

The pounding started up again.

"Coming, Officer," he shouted above the din. "I'm unarmed and opening the door now, so hold your fire."

He turned the lock and started to swing the door open. It exploded inward, and two officers were on him in an instant, tossing him to the bed and pinning him there. A third started to cuff him. Wade lay there quietly, wondering if the judge would take his cooperative attitude into account when handing down his sentence.

"Would someone please explain to me what the hell is going on here?"

All three officers froze midaction at Tanya's imperious tone, and then stared blankly as she stalked in from the bathroom, head high in the air. In spite of his predicament, Wade smothered a chuckle in the pillows. She was quite a sight with her half wet hair, bandaged head and white towel knotted at the waist over her hospital greens. No wonder the men appeared taken aback by her sudden appearance.

The officer with the handcuffs recovered first. "Are you Tanya Riverton?" he asked.

"Yes, Officer, I am. And who might you be?"

"I'm Detective Greg Jansen of the Bellevue Police Department, ma'am. We're here to liberate you from your kidnapper."

"Kidnapper? Gentlemen, please. This man rescued me. He deserves a medal for his bravery. Now release him this instant." The two officers eyed each other uncertainly.

"Now!" she demanded.

They let go immediately and backed away from the bed. Wade felt sorry for them. He knew that tone.

"Rescued you from what?" Jansen asked.

"From the man who tried to chloroform me in my hospital room."

"And what was Mr. Scott doing in your hospital room, Ms. Riverton."

"I was protecting her," Wade interjected.

Jansen glanced briefly in his direction, before turning back to Tanya. "Is he a friend of yours, Ms. Riverton?"

"Yes," she responded smoothly, surprising herself at how easy the lie came out. "In fact, he's a very good friend, Detective."

"I see. Ms. Riverton, although we found evidence of chloroform in your room, we didn't find anyone else there."

"I chased the guy out of the room. He disappeared, but I couldn't be sure that he wouldn't come back again. That's why I brought Tanya here."

The detective glanced briefly in Wade's direction, favoring him with a disbelieving look before he turned back to Tanya. "Why would someone want to attack you, Ms. Riverton?"

She glanced at Wade uncertainly, who shrugged.

"I'm not entirely sure, Detective Jansen."

"Did someone also attack you in your apartment yesterday afternoon?"

Her eyes again sought Wade's help, but he only shrugged again.

"I don't know."

"What do you mean, you don't know?"

"Well, I have this little memory problem, you see. Everything prior to just over an hour ago is a complete blank."

"But you remember Mr. Scott."

"Not exactly."

Jansen gave her a look that spoke volumes. "You're telling me you have no idea who this guy is, yet you're buying his story? How do you know he wasn't the one who dropped the chloroform on the floor after administering it to you? How do you know this man wasn't trying to kill you at your apartment yesterday afternoon and then again at the hospital last night?"

Tanya glanced at Wade briefly, before rolling her eyes skyward. "I'm still alive, aren't I?" she informed the detective, sarcasm dripping off every word.

Wade nearly laughed aloud at the look on Jansen's face. The man was clearly furious. He started to respond to her remark and then changed his mind, deciding that Wade should bear the brunt of his frustration instead. "I think maybe I'll run you in anyway, Scott."

"What's the charge, Officer?"

"Kidnapping, for starters. We'll see what else turns up. Hit any more cops lately?"

"Kidnapping?" Tanya cut in. "Who did he kidnap, Detective?"

"You, Ms. Riverton."

"Me? Do I look kidnapped to you, Wade, darling?"

"Not at all, sweetheart."

"You were unconscious at the time, ma'am. He removed you from your hospital room without your consent, or the consent of your attending physician."

"Well, if I were awake, I would have given him my consent."

Wade heard a small choking sound behind him and swiveled his head toward the two officers who had originally pinned him down. He smiled knowingly at the bemused expression on their faces.

"You'd better tell your friend to give it up. She's like a dog with a bone when she gets going. How did you guys find me, anyway?"

"Hospital security video," one of them muttered quietly.

Jansen spun around to glare at his backup team who snapped guiltily to attention, their faces immediately reflecting cool, professional detachment. He tossed one more ferocious stare in Wade's direction before turning back to Tanya. "I'll need you to come down to the station and file a report, Ms. Riverton. Would you come with me, please?"

"Like this?" she asked incredulously.

"She has no clothing with her, sir. Why don't I bring her down to the station once we find something for her to wear," Wade suggested.

Jansen hesitated a moment, and then apparently thought better of what he had been about to say. "Fine. Just make sure it's before five o'clock this afternoon." He motioned for the other officers to leave and moved after them, pausing a moment in the doorway to glance back at Wade. "One more thing. Why didn't you just take her home?"

"Because that's exactly where the assassin would look for her next."

Jansen raised one eyebrow in disbelief. "I'll be watching you, Scott," he warned as he closed the door behind him.

Chapter Three

"You owe me," Tanya advised in a coolly superior tone as soon as the police had left.

"Yeah, I guess I do," Wade admitted. "Thanks for your help with the detective."

"You're welcome. But what did he mean, have you hit any more cops recently?"

He shrugged. "It was a heat of the moment thing. I don't usually make a habit of it."

"Heat of the moment? What happened?"

"The cop insulted my sister, and I took a swing at him. No big deal, really, except of course to him. Now, let's get you into some proper clothes." He took the bottle of aspirin she still held in her hand and tucked it back into his pocket before picking up his leather jacket from the back of the chair and handing it to her. "Why don't you put this on while we're in the truck?"

"Okay. Thanks." She accepted the jacket from him and slipped it on over her shoulders, inhaling appreciatively the clean, masculine scent of his aftershave. "Wait a minute. You never did explain why someone wanted to assassinate me in the hospital last night."

Wade hesitated, wondering how much to tell her. As little as possible for the moment, he decided. Until he could form some sort of action plan, he did not want to tip his hand.

"Well, maybe it had something to do with that private investigator you hired. Cliff Peterson. I guess you probably won't remember this either, but he was blown up in his office on the weekend."

Her blank look of astonishment confirmed the truth of his last statement. "Blown up?"

"Yes. The blast wiped out almost the entire office building. Destroyed all his records completely."

"Why did I hire him?"

"You never said."

"I never told you why I had hired a private investigator?"

Wade shrugged. "You told me it was none of my business." Or at least that was what she would have said had he asked. And no doubt have put it a lot more eloquently than that, he added to himself, turning away to hide the tiny smile tugging at the corner of his mouth. Which seemed to be her style of dealing with everyone, if the way she had gone directly for the detective's jugular a few moments ago was any indication. At least he knew now not to take her sharp tongue quite so personally. Apparently, she was not particular about who was on the receiving end of one of her bloodthirsty tirades.

"None of your business?" she repeated, puzzled by his words.

"C'mon. Let's go." Wade grabbed his keys from the back pocket of his jeans and moved toward the door, hoping to distract her present train of thought. He knew from experience she had the most irritating tendency to belabor an issue to death once she warmed to her subject, and so he was not about to give her an opportunity to say anything further on the matter. He opened the door and turned back to her. "After you," he motioned gallantly.

She took a couple of steps toward the door and then stopped short, frowning.

"What's wrong?"

"I don't know where I live. And even if I managed to figure it out, I don't have any keys to get into the place. Unless . . . do we live together?"

He shook his head, and Tanya felt a small stab of disappointment.

"But I do have a set of keys to your apartment. So you're in luck."

"Great." Outwardly, her manner was nonchalant, but inside her stomach was a swirling mass of sudden nerves. If he had keys to her apartment, they must know each other well. Perhaps intimately. What kind of memories dwelt in the dark void that had swallowed up all recollection of her past life history? What sort of pleasures might the two of them have shared?

"Ouch." She winced in pain as she climbed up into the passenger seat of Wade's truck. After the excitement of the police visit, she'd temporarily forgotten what her body had been through yesterday, but now, her complaining muscles were an effective reminder of her need to take it easy for a few days.

Wade slipped behind the wheel and promptly grunted in pain himself. He fished into his right front pocket and pulled out the aspirin bottle. "I almost forgot," he told Tanya as he opened the glove box and tossed the aspirin inside. "I always keep a bottle handy," he added, in response to her questioning look. "I came and got them while you were in the shower."

Tanya sat quietly on her side of the truck, her mind busily trying to sift through a jumble of confusing thoughts. She kept coming back to the million-dollar unanswered question: what was the exact nature of her relationship with Wade Scott? And found herself hoping that they were as close as he'd implied earlier. For that brief moment when he was going to kiss her, she had felt as if nothing in the world mattered save for the touch of his lips, except perhaps the feel of his impressively muscled body pressing tightly against hers.

Then it hadn't seemed to matter at all that she'd no clue who she was, no idea where she was, and no way of knowing if her feminine intuition was right or not. Despite Detective Jansen's doubts about Wade, her own instinct was to believe in him, to trust that his hard strength would protect her and make everything in her topsy-turvy world all right again. There was an air about him, an aura of trustworthiness and integrity that told her no matter what the circumstances, she could depend on him.

And yet by his own admission, she had told him it was none of his business why she'd hired a private investigator. Perhaps it was Wade himself she was having investigated. What if she were wrong about the big man who was accompanying her to her apartment? From the size and strength of his hands resting so calmly and capably on the steering wheel, she knew that should he turn on her, she would stand no chance of escape. Her body shifted restlessly at that disturbing thought.

"You're very quiet."

"I'm thinking."

"About what?"

"About everything I know nothing about," she complained. "You, me, my life, my family . . . " Her voice trailed off as another disturbing thought struck her. "Do I have children?" she asked hesitantly.

"Nope, no kids," he answered, flashing her a quick smile before turning his eyes back to the road in front of him.

"Oh." She wasn't sure whether to feel relieved or disappointed by the knowledge.

"It must be rough," he sympathized. "Not being able to remember anything, I mean. For the record, you're twenty-six years old. And an only child. Your mother lives in Bellingham, a couple of hours drive from where you live here in Bellevue, just outside of Seattle. You grew up in Bellevue; your mother moved away only a few years ago. Does any of this sound at all familiar to you?"

She shook her head, sighing with frustration. "No. Say," she added, brightening a little, "perhaps if I went to visit my mother it might jog my memory."

Uh oh. That was definitely not a good plan. Although Tanya might not have any idea who he was, her mother would have no trouble at all remembering him. And then the cat would certainly be out of the bag. One look at him and Tanya's mother would quickly quash any hope of him using whatever information was locked away inside her daughter's head to find Cliff's murderer. It was time for some quick thinking.

"We could pay her a visit," he began doubtfully, "but we might be putting her in unnecessary danger. If whoever is after you suspects your mother knows anything at all, she could well be his next target."

"Oh, I guess you're right." She paused a moment and then asked, "What about my father?"

Wade frowned. "He died a number of years ago."

"What happened?"

Wade paused as he turned right onto 156th Avenue. "It was an industrial accident," he explained after successfully negotiating the turn. "You were about fourteen at the time, I believe. It was pretty hard on you. You and your father were quite close. Anyway, after high school, you attended North Seattle Community College. After that, you worked for the city for a couple of years, and then recently you went to work for Pacific Realtors."

He glanced at her once again, checking her expression for any sign of recollection. But the only thing reflecting in her face was the same blank stare of confusion. Wade felt his body relax, and for the first time he allowed himself to believe that his little charade might actually work. If all went well, he would be in and out of her life before she figured out who he was.

"Well, here we are," he announced as he turned into the Central Park East complex, hoping that the fortuitous timing of their arrival at her apartment building would forestall any further questioning on her part. "You're in suite number eight, third floor."

"I fell three stories?" she asked, surprised. Her eyes counted the rows of balconies from one to three. An involuntary shudder passed through her body. It was quite a distance up, and consequently, a correspondingly long way down from the top rail of her balcony to the solid, unyielding earth below.

"That's right. You were very lucky. Those bushes at the base of the building over there broke your fall."

Wade pulled into the visitor's parking and cut the engine. He took a look at her apprehensive face and unexpectedly felt a surge of sympathy. Irritating blonde or not, the woebegone expression in her eyes made her look so uncharacteristically vulnerable that he couldn't stop his heart from softening just a wee bit. Despite his earlier resolve to keep the boyfriend impersonation thing strictly business, he captured her hand in his and squeezed reassuringly. "Don't worry. I'm here for you."

She smiled weakly and opened the passenger door.

They approached the front entrance.

"Your keys are in the inside pocket of my jacket."

She reached inside his jacket to retrieve the keys and stared down at them, noting that her hand was trembling slightly. At least, the shaky grip was matching perfectly with the fluttering of her insides, she acknowledged to herself with grim amusement. It was only her feet that were solid and unmoving, rooting her firmly to the spot as she struggled with a sudden case of nerves. What would she find behind the door of suite 308? Answers, or simply more questions? Would she like what she found, or would the truth of who she was be a disappointment to her? Squaring her shoulders, she tried several keys from the key ring until one turned obligingly in the lock. Taking a strong, steadying breath, she pushed open the door.

There was one benefit in not knowing her past. Right now, the present was wide open, and she could be anyone she wanted. Including Wade's girlfriend. The idea certainly held appeal. She studied his back as she followed him into the elevator, admiring the way the broad V of his wide shoulders tapered to a trim waist and tight buns. He looked as good from behind as he did face on.

The elevator door opened on the third floor. She stared out into the hall, her body again immobile as her mind struggled with the uncertainty of what lay ahead. Wade placed his arm around her shoulders and, with gentle pressure, encouraged her forward. She relaxed against the warmth of his body and allowed him to take charge.

The door to her apartment rested slightly ajar. Tanya glanced at her companion apprehensively. He frowned, equally concerned.

"Wait here," he ordered, pressing her back against the wall and out of any possible line of fire.

She watched as he slowly pushed the door open and cautiously stepped into the room. She stood motionless, scarcely breathing, all her senses alert for any clue as to what was happening inside. Not a single sound broke the heavy silence. The wait was interminable. What on earth was he doing in there?

At long last, Wade reappeared in the doorway. "You'd better come inside," he suggested, his face grim.

She entered the apartment and stared about her in dismay. The place was a disaster. Books and photographs from her wall unit were strewn across the living room floor, and even the cushions had been removed from her couch and tossed into the centre of the room. The jewel boxes of her CD collection had all been opened up, and dozens of shiny discs were piled up on the carpet in front of her stereo system. All of her potted plants had been turned upside down.

The kitchen drawers had been removed from their slots, and their contents upended on the linoleum floor. Pots, pans, and dozens of broken dishes had joined them there. The garbage from her waste container was spread about. Boxes of cereal and other dry goods had also been emptied onto the floor.

Rallying against the sinking sensation in the pit of her stomach, she took a deep, calming breath and walked down the short hallway toward the far end of the apartment. The bedroom and bathroom were in no better shape, with clothing and other personal items scattered across both rooms. The mattress from her bed had been lifted up and flipped onto the floor.

"It looks like whoever it was picked the lock."

Tanya started, so engrossed in her examination of the total devastation that she'd been completely oblivious to Wade's approach.

"Great," she sighed. "Now what?"

"I guess we talk to the police again."

Tanya changed into appropriate clothing, careful to disturb as little in the room as possible. She and Wade sat quietly at the kitchen table until the police arrived. Conversation was sporadic at best, with both of them distracted by their own personal thoughts, each wondering privately what was really going on.

The two responding officers were veterans at break-and-enter cases, their analysis quick yet thorough as they dusted for fingerprints and collected their evidence. Before long, their investigation was complete.

"I doubt we'll find much," one of the officers advised apologetically as he and his partner were getting ready to leave. "The way the lock was picked, I'd say whoever did this was a professional. And obviously looking for something. You're sure you have no idea what they could have been after?"

"I wish I did," Tanya sighed. "But until my memory comes back, your guess is as good as mine."

After the officers left, Wade drove Tanya to the hospital where they both apologized profusely to the disapproving staff for Tanya's impromptu departure the night before. Wade took care of the bill, while Tanya sat quietly in the corner, struggling to cope with the utter exhaustion which had suddenly overtaken her body. The adrenaline that had kept her going to this point had run dry, so that now all she wanted to do was close her eyes for a short while to get some of the healing rest her aching body so desperately needed.

The bill paid, Wade strolled over to where Tanya was fighting to keep her eyes open and sat down beside her. She started slightly as he placed a small gray purse in her lap.

"You were lying on top of this when the ambulance crew picked you up," he told her quietly. "That must mean your exit from the apartment balcony was deliberate. Why else would you have had your purse with you?"

Tanya frowned as she slowly digested this newest piece of information. Too much was happening, and it was happening much too fast for her to make sense of it.

"Why would I want to jump off my apartment balcony?" she wondered aloud.

"Someone might have been trying to come through the door," Wade offered. "C'mon, let's get out of here. Maybe there's something in your purse that can help us figure this thing out."

Tanya examined the contents of her purse as Wade drove her to the police station so that she could file her report with Detective Jansen. She opened her wallet, which contained her driver's license, a couple of credit cards, a bank card, several charge slips, a few grocery coupons, and approximately $50 cash. The only other items included a cell phone, a tube of lipstick, a hairbrush, and a silver pen. Disappointment flared, and Tanya bit back the urge to scream in frustration. In terms of figuring out who she was, it certainly wasn't much to go on.

Wade dropped her off in front of police headquarters at City Hall, telling her he had some business to take care of but would be back to pick her up by the time she was done with the paperwork.

True to his word, he was reading a magazine in the front lobby when Tanya emerged from the interior offices an hour and a half later.

"Were you waiting long?" she asked as he held the main door open for her.

"Not really. I knew you were going to be a while. How did it go in there?"

She made a face. "Detective Jansen was his usual charming self. He made me feel like a criminal for not being able to remember anything that happened to me yesterday. He got really angry that I didn't call him personally about the break in. I, of course, reminded him that his manner wasn't exactly conducive to us being buddies."

"Of course," Wade agreed, grinning. He suspected their conversation had rapidly degenerated from that point on.

"He actually suggested I might be in on the whole thing," she added indignantly.

"What whole thing?" he asked, a frown of concern quickly replacing his amused expression.

"Beats me," she shrugged.

They climbed into the truck and headed back to her apartment. Tanya fell into a brooding silence, the stress of the day finally overwhelming her. She was exhausted, and more than a little depressed. Her poor body was bruised and hurting, and the thought of facing the huge clean up job ahead of her was causing her sagging spirits to drop even further.

Once he'd pulled into visitor's parking at the apartment complex, Wade reached back into the crew seat and lifted out a couple of plastic bags.

"What do you have there?"

"Garbage bags, paper plates, and plastic cups, for starters. I also picked up a better quality dead bolt, and a heavier chain lock. I want to install them right away to make sure you're safe."

"Thanks." She felt a warm glow wash over her as she acknowledged his thoughtfulness. It felt nice to be taken care of, especially after the kind of day she'd woken up to. Her gloomy outlook brightened a little.

Once upstairs, Wade immediately got to work installing the new locks while Tanya busied herself tidying up the kitchen. A good portion of glassware and dishes ended up in the garbage, along with most of her packaged food. Moving slowly to pacify her protesting muscles, it took quite a while to sort through it all.

"I'm hungry," she announced as Wade finished up with the door. "What do you want to do for food?"

"What about pizza?" he asked. "After the day you've had, I doubt you'll want to mess around in the kitchen. Besides, I'm not sure what still might be edible in there."

"Sounds great. I think I saw a phone book on the floor in the living room. Why don't you order it. I'm sure you know what I like better than me. Although I do seem to recall I hate pineapple on pizza."

"No problem." He located the phone book and made the call. "Do you mind if I take a quick shower before the pizza arrives?"

"Yeah, sure. Help yourself."

Wade rubbed his chin. "I wish I had my razor with me."

"Use one of mine. So they're pink instead of blue," she added at his look of surprise. "Big deal. There's a bag of them underneath the sink in the bathroom."

She headed into the living room to tackle the mess there, but then stopped short and rushed toward the bathroom instead. Her shout of triumph carried out into the hallway.

"What is it?"

"They're here! The bag of razors is under the sink, just as I pictured it. I remembered something, Wade."

She glanced up from where she was kneeling on the bathroom floor as Wade poked his head inside the bathroom. "There's hope for me yet," she told him, her eyes sparkling with excitement.

Tanya jumped to her feet and rushed out into the hallway toward the linen closet. "And here are the towels." She picked one up off the floor from where the intruder had tossed it and handed it to him. "They're pink. I knew they would be pink."

"That's great. Maybe with a good night's sleep, it'll all come back to you by morning," he offered encouragingly, all the while praying that wouldn't be the case.

Wade helped himself to one of the razors and turned on the water. Tanya's memory recall didn't bode well for him. Minor though the incidents might be, they were still a warning to him that her full memory could return at any time. He had to find what he needed as quickly as he could and then get the hell out of her apartment.

Had the person or persons who demolished the place earlier beat him to the punch? There was no way of knowing for sure. The only thing he could do was hang around until something else happened. Something would, and soon. Of that he was certain, for whoever had killed Cliff had gone to a lot of time, trouble, and expense to blow up his office building, while simultaneously framing both Cliff and Janie for drug trafficking. The setup was obviously a ruse to send the police on a wild goose chase while the real evidence trail grew cold. With so much clearly at stake, these people wouldn't risk allowing Tanya to live. He had to find out what information was locked away in that confused little brain of hers before they got to her, for he was convinced that her life, and now likely his, depended on it.

How long would it take Jansen to link him to Cliff? he wondered. The detective struck him as someone who would stubbornly sniff around until he eventually found something. Did the man really believe Tanya was involved in some way?

Wade himself seriously doubted it. Though she was often a royal pain in the butt, he found it hard to believe she could be a criminal. Besides,

Cliff had hinted that Tanya had originally approached him because she was suspicious of someone else's activities. If only Cliff had told him who that someone had been.

There was always the possibility that Tanya would continue to work with him once her memory returned, but he rather doubted it. She'd already made a career out of tormenting him and was stubborn enough to continue that path, even though he might be her only ally in a potentially deadly situation.

Wade shut the water off and began to towel himself dry. Worrying about the situation wasn't going to solve anything. He would just have to stay alert and watch for any and all possible clues.

A knock at the door caused him to stiffen in concern. He heard her call to the person in the outside hallway and grabbed frantically for his jeans. Surely, she would not open the door while he was still in the bathroom?

He wrenched open the bathroom door and raced down the hallway, just in time to see Tanya offering the money he'd left on the counter to a young kid holding a box of pizza.

He attacked the moment she shut the door.

"Are you crazy? Don't ever open the door again unless I'm here to protect you."

She gaped at him, startled by his unexpected fury. "But it was just the pizza guy," she protested.

"And how did you know that?" Wade demanded angrily.

She pointed to the telephone on the wall. "He called up for me to buzz him in."

"Oh." Wade felt a little foolish as his initial rush of adrenaline subsided. "Well, even so, you never know."

"Do you really think someone would go to the trouble of bugging my phone and then impersonating a delivery man in order to get into this apartment?" Tanya was more curious than angered by the high-handed manner in which he'd just called her crazy. Actually, she was rather pleased by his obvious concern for her safety.

She stared appreciatively at his bare chest, the softly curling hair in the centre of it still damp with tiny water droplets. The mass of curls narrowed as it continued downward, traversing the length of his stomach and disappearing underneath the waistband of his jeans. Minus the T-shirt, his muscles were every bit as large and hard as the tight-fitting garment had alluded earlier.

His beard was gone, she noted, liking what she saw. His freshly shaved face gave him a boyish look, which most definitely added to his charm.

She also liked the way his damp hair curled slightly at the ends as it just skimmed the top of his shoulders.

"You never know," he mumbled awkwardly, uncomfortably aware of her appraising stare.

All of a sudden, he was acutely conscious of the fact that they were very much alone in her apartment. He remembered how he'd been drawn against his will to kiss her earlier this morning and swallowed hard. It was going to be a long evening, for he was determined to keep his distance and yet keep a close eye on her at the same time.

"Let's eat," he announced abruptly, taking the pizza box from her and placing it on the counter. "Where are those paper plates?"

They settled themselves at the kitchen table and dug in. Tanya found cans of pop in the fridge, and so they washed their pizza down with Diet Coke. Both of them were hungry, and the pizza disappeared quickly.

Her stomach comfortably full, a wave of utter exhaustion overtook her, and she was suddenly overwhelmed by how tired she felt. "I think I need to go to bed," she announced, yawning. She looked at the clock on the microwave. "It's only eight o'clock, but it feels like I've been up all night."

"Go ahead. I think I'll watch some TV for a while."

She stared at him, an unspoken question in her eyes.

"I hope you don't mind if I stay the night," he added, in response to her look of inquiry. "I really think it would be better if I stayed just in case whoever was here earlier comes back later on tonight."

"No problem." She really didn't mind in the least if he stayed. In fact, she was rather glad of his offer, for the thought of being alone in the dark in a strange place was a little alarming, even if she was in her own apartment. It was debatable whether anyone would return to the scene of their crime so quickly, but nonetheless, she felt much safer knowing Wade would be here. Just in case.

The real question in her mind was not whether he should stay, but rather where exactly he was going to sleep. Should she offer him a blanket and pillow for the couch, or was he assuming he would crawl into bed with her later on? Was that a normal occurrence in their relationship? She knew she should probably ask, but the thought of raising such an intimate question was embarrassing. She decided instead to play it by ear and see what happened.

Leaving Wade to pick up the remains of their dinner, she quickly washed her face and brushed her teeth before crawling thankfully into bed. She was out like a light, asleep almost before her head hit the pillow.

After putting the living room back into some semblance of order, Wade settled himself in front of the television, flipping absently through the channels. He had little interest in the mindless entertainment flickering across the screen. What he really wanted was a look at the local news, to see if any additional details were being reported about the circumstances surrounding Cliff's death.

It was now 8:30, and it appeared he had an hour and a half to kill before any of the news programs began to air. He gave up playing with the remote control and settled on one of the more popular sitcoms. Though the program wasn't particularly to his liking, it would help pass the time, if nothing else.

Bored with the senseless dialogue of the television program, his mind began to wander of its own accord. He thought about Cliff, remembering the numbing shock he'd experienced upon receiving the news of his death, and his subsequent outrage at the accusations being made by the local police detachment. As ridiculous as it seemed, it appeared they were buying the drug setup, and Wade had to find the evidence to prove his brother-in-law's innocence and restore his reputation. The last thing he wanted was for Cliff's kids to grow up believing their father was a criminal.

At the moment, Tanya was his only lead, and all he had to go on was a casual conversation he'd shared with Cliff barely a week ago. Cliff had mentioned he was doing some investigative work for Tanya Riverton, and the two of them had laughed at the thought of how mad she would have been if she'd had any idea the two of them were related, even if only by marriage. Cliff had also hinted that Tanya may have stumbled onto something big and that he himself might be in over his head. But that was all he'd shared on the matter.

And now Tanya was in grave danger. Cliff was dead, and Wade was certain that whoever had come after Tanya wouldn't stop until she was in the same condition. His association with her probably made him a target as well. However, that was a risk he was prepared to take in order to discover the truth and clear his brother-in-law's name.

A piercing scream from the end of the hallway brought him to his feet, heart in his throat. How could anyone have got past him? He flew down the hallway, and exploded into the bedroom, hackles raised, fists cocked and ready.

Tanya sat huddled in the center of the bed, the covers wrapped protectively around her, her face wet with tears. Wade glanced frantically about the room, searching high and low for the enemy.

"What happened?" he demanded.

"I had the most horrible dream," she whimpered.

He expelled his breath with an angry whoosh that echoed harshly in the tiny room. "You scared the hell out of me, Tanya."

"I-I'm s-s-sorry," she apologized, and promptly burst into a fresh round of tears.

Wade sat down on the edge of the bed. "It's okay," he soothed, patting her shoulder awkwardly. "Don't worry about it. Tell me about the dream."

"I can't r-r-remember," she blubbered. "I'm s-sorry. I feel like s-such an i-idiot, but I c-can't s-seem to s-s-stop c-c-crying."

With a sigh of helpless resignation, he gathered her into his arms. She rested her brow against his chest and he began to softly stroke her hair, whispering gentle words of encouragement. "It's okay. It was just a dream. As long as I'm here, no one is going to hurt you."

She remained in the comfort of his warm embrace for several minutes, needing him to hold her. It had been one hell of a day, spiraling from bad to worse with each passing hour. The dream had been the last straw, the one that had caused her overstretched nerves to finally snap. Now all she wanted to do was hide her head on Wade's broad shoulder in order to escape from the living nightmare her life had become. His touch was soothing, his body reassuringly hard, and right now she needed to draw upon his gentle strength to make it through the night.

At long last Tanya reluctantly pulled herself away from his body. "Thanks," she gulped, looking up at him with a watery smile.

He smiled back. "No problem," he told her, his tone gently reassuring. "Anytime."

Their eyes met and locked. It grew suddenly very warm in the room, and the muscles constricting in the center of her chest made it difficult for Tanya to breathe. Her heart stopped beating for a split second as she registered the way Wade was looking at her and recognized the meaning of it with the instinctive knowing of a woman's intuition. She knew exactly what he was feeling, for she felt it too.

Wade stared down at the delicate flower he was cradling in his arms. At the moment, she felt as fragile as a newly opening blossom, and her skin looked as soft and smooth as a rose petal freshly kissed by the morning dew. He breathed in her sweet scent, noticing that her hair smelled faintly like the lilac bushes which bloomed so fragrantly in his mother's garden every year.

He swallowed hard, wanting more than anything at that particular moment to kiss her. She was bewitching in this rare moment of vulnerability, and the spell she was presently weaving so tightly around his emotions had him teetering precariously on the thin line between control and abandonment, with control definitely on the losing side.

Yes, they were both adults, but one of them was here under false pretences. Namely him. So what kind of bastard would he be if he took advantage of the situation, other than a very human one? He continued to look at her, captivated by the way her eyes glowed luminously in the darkened room, the light from the hallway reflecting off her pupils, shiny with unshed tears. The inviting expression on her face was too much for him to bear, and with a groan, he reached down to brush his lips against hers in a tender kiss.

She responded at once, wrapping her arms around his neck and lifting her face up closer to him. Their kiss deepened, and as his lips grew more and more demanding, she responded just as eagerly. When they finally came up for air, she murmured softly and nibbled gently at the side of his neck. He groaned again, crushing her to him.

She whimpered in pain, and he immediately relaxed his hold. "Sorry, sweetheart," he apologized as he lowered her carefully onto the surface of the bed and drew his own body along side hers.

"It's okay, Wade," she murmured back, tracing the outline of his mouth with her index finger.

"I'd forgotten how sore you must be after the fall you took."

"Don't worry about it. Just kiss me again."

He obliged, and she surrendered herself once again to the wonderful sensations coursing throughout every inch of her body. She tugged his T-shirt from the waistband of his jeans and slipped her hand underneath it, wanting very badly to touch him. He opened the top few buttons of her night gown, and she arched encouragingly toward him, moaning with pleasure as he began to caress first one breast, and then the other.

He paused unexpectedly after a moment, and she opened her eyes to find him staring at her uncertainly.

"Are you okay to . . . ?"

She nodded.

"Are you sure?" he asked one more time, the last ounce of gentleman in him forcing him to offer her an out, even as his baser self knew that an answer in the negative would kill him.

She nodded again. "Just watch my ribs," she whispered with a teasing smile.

Chapter Four

A fierce pounding on the door startled them both awake. Wade was on his feet in an instant, struggling with his jeans. Tanya snatched up her dressing gown, a sudden adrenaline surge momentarily overshadowing the jab of pain from her bruised ribs.

Wade reached the door first and peered through the security view hole. "What the . . . ?" he muttered, frowning.

"Let me see." She brushed past him to take a peek. Detective Jansen was fidgeting impatiently in the hallway, his hand raised and about to knock again. "Hold on," she called out, starting to undo the locks.

Jansen marched into the room without waiting to be invited, ignoring her polite "good morning."

"Why didn't you tell me Cliff Peterson was your brother-in-law?" he demanded, fixing Wade with a hostile glare.

"You never asked."

"What kind of a goddamn answer is that, Scott?"

"It's the goddamn truth, Jansen."

"You deliberately withheld relevant information."

"What's so relevant about it?"

"Your brother-in-law gets blown up in his office from an explosion big enough to wipe out three entire floors, and then your friend here is attacked in the hospital. What if these incidents are connected in some way? Or maybe you don't want me to make the connection," he added, his eyes narrowing suspiciously. "What are you hiding, Scott?"

"I'm not hiding anything, Detective. I just don't think my relationship to Peterson is all that important."

"Is that right? Well, you want to know what I think, Scott? I think you're involved in all this, and you're using Ms. Riverton for something. I just don't know what for yet."

"That's ridiculous."

"What about the money and drugs we found at the Peterson residence? Were you in on part of that deal? Are you a goddamn drug dealer too?"

"You son-of-a-bitch!" Wade grabbed Jansen by the front of his shirt with both hands and slammed him against the wall.

Tanya leaped between the two men, pressing back on Wade's chest with all the force she could muster. It was like pushing against a brick wall. "Wade, stop it this instant. I mean it!"

His hold never slackened. The two men stared at each other. Though neither said a word, both men's eyes issued a silent challenge.

She tugged on Wade's ear gently. "Hey," she whispered softly, "can you hear me in there?"

In spite of his anger, a small smile tugged at the corner of his mouth. "Yes, I hear you, Tanya," he answered, still glaring at Jansen.

"Good. Now don't hit the nice cop, Wade. He's just doing his job."

Wade sighed, and she felt his body relax. "Okay, Tanya, I won't hit the nice cop. But he better get the hell out of here quick."

Tanya turned to the detective. "You heard the man. Now take your testosterone and vacate the premises, Detective Jansen, before I lose my temper."

"Better do as the lady says," Wade warned, stepping back a pace as he let go of Jansen's shirt. "Unless, of course, you have a search warrant."

"Not yet. But that can always be arranged." Jansen straightened his shirt, smoothing out the stretch marks Wade's fingers had imprinted in the material. He glanced once more at Tanya. "Be very careful who you take into your confidence, Ms. Riverton." Then with a brief nod of his head, he disappeared out into the hallway.

Tanya shut the door and whirled on Wade, a hurricane of fury. "You never told me Cliff Peterson was your brother-in-law. Why not? Money and drugs? What the hell was he talking about? Are you involved? And where do I fit in?" She gasped as another possibility struck her. "Had we even met before yesterday?"

"Yes. Many times," he acknowledged.

"So how did we meet?"

"We went to school together."

"Really?" The tone of her voice suggested that she wasn't sure whether to believe him.

"Really," he assured her. "Look, I saw a school yearbook on the living room floor yesterday. I'll prove it to you."

She walked into the living room and glanced quickly through the books Wade had placed into her wall unit the previous evening. After several moments of searching, she retrieved the yearbook and handed it to Wade.

He opened it and flipped quickly through the pages, pausing approximately halfway through the volume. "See. There we are on these two opposite pages," he commented, returning the book to her. "Riverton and Scott. We were in the same graduating class."

She stared at the pages without speaking. A few seconds later, she snapped the book shut. "Okay, but that still doesn't explain why you didn't tell me about you and Cliff."

"I didn't want to frighten you," he explained. "Especially when I don't even know for sure what else Cliff may have been involved with. I know he and Janie were having their problems, but she won't tell me anything about it. Besides, everything was happening so quickly, I . . . there wasn't much of a chance to tell you about it anyway."

She returned the book to its place on the shelf. Sighing loudly, she faced him again, arms crossed in front of her chest. "I have to ask this. Last night . . . had we ever done that before?"

His face flushed. "No," he told her quietly, averting his eyes.

"I see. Then how well *do* we know each other?"

"Not very," he admitted in the same subdued tone.

"Then how is it you had my apartment keys? Were you here yesterday when I "fell" off the balcony?"

"No," he was quick to assure her. "But I was pulling into the visitor's parking lot just as you came tumbling down the side of the building. Considering what had just happened to Cliff, I wondered if perhaps someone had pushed you. So after I made sure you were still breathing all right on your own and told another witness to call 911, I quickly climbed up the side of the balconies and into your apartment to check things out. There was no one here, and everything seemed okay, so I found your keys and left through the front door. I had planned to tell you this when I went to see you in the hospital, and then hand you your keys so you could get back into your apartment once you were ready to go home."

"So why didn't you tell me this yesterday?"

"Well, you didn't remember anything, and then things got a little complicated."

"A little complicated . . . ?"

"Well, take last night for instance." He took a step toward her, a sexy grin curving the corners of his mouth as his eyes glowed in renewed invitation.

"Don't you touch me," she ordered, moving backward.

He raised an eyebrow as the smile slowly faded. "It's a little late for that, don't you think?"

"I didn't know what I was doing," she countered, her tone defensive.

"Yeah? I think you knew damn well what you were doing, Tanya."

She glared back at him. "Get out of here. I don't want to ever see you again."

"Forget it. I'm not going anywhere. You need me."

"Hah!"

"People are after you. You don't know who they are, and you have no idea why they want you. I'm the only one you can trust."

"So what? I'll just use the police."

"You think Jansen is going to care what happens to you after the way you just treated him?"

She paused, knowing he was right, but not wanting to admit it. Common sense, along with a growing desire not to see him go, finally won out over pride. "Okay, but from now on, it's strictly business."

"Fine by me. Partners?" he asked, holding out his hand.

"Partners." She took his hand, thus sealing their bargain. "So now are you going to tell me exactly what's going on? I'll make some coffee," she added as he nodded.

Wade admired the way her cute little derriere swayed back and forth as she made her way into the kitchen, fighting the temptation to take her back to bed. It was a shame that they wouldn't be frolicking under the bed sheets again in this lifetime. Tanya had made that perfectly clear. Not that he blamed her, under the circumstances.

He shook his head to clear away the carnal thoughts. He should be trying to find Cliff's killer, not allowing his libido free license to fantasize about making love to sexy little Tanya Riverton.

"And put some clothes on," she shouted irritably from the kitchen.

Wade glanced down at his bare chest and grinned. It was nice to know she found him distracting too.

The telephone rang.

Tanya stuck her face through the kitchen door, eyeing the phone on the wall warily. She then glanced at Wade. "Why don't you answer that and find out who it is. I don't think I want anyone to know I have amnesia at the moment."

"Good idea." He reached for the phone. "Hello?"

"Oh," said a surprised feminine voice at the other end of the line. "Is Tanya there?"

"Who may I say is calling?"

"It's Sandra."

"Yes?" He waited, hoping his expectant silence would encourage the woman to say more.

"I work with her . . . at the office . . . ," Sandra continued, a little hesitantly.

"Okay. Just a minute."

He placed his hand over the mouth piece and turned to Tanya. "It's Sandra, from the office."

"Thanks." She took the phone from him and lifted the receiver to her ear. "Hello, Sandra."

"Tanya. Thank God! Are you okay? I heard you fell from the balcony of your apartment."

"Yes, but don't worry. I'm fine. Just a few bruises."

There was a short, uncomfortable pause.

"Uh, how's things at the office?"

"Oh. Everything's okay. Dave thought you might want to take a few days off. You know, until you're feeling a bit better."

"Yes, I think that would probably be a good idea," Tanya confirmed, wondering who the heck Dave was.

"Are you okay, Tanya?" Sandra sounded genuinely concerned. "You were so upset when you left the office yesterday, and you still sound kind of strange."

"Oh, it was no big deal," she replied carelessly. "I got everything taken care of."

"Well, all right then. But if you need to talk to someone, you just let me know."

"Thanks, Sandra. I'll keep that in mind."

"You never told me you had a boyfriend," the other woman blurted. "But then, you're a very private person. Besides, if he's the guy who came by the office to see you yesterday after you'd already left, I'm not surprised you've been keeping him to yourself. What a hunk!"

"What was his name?"

"He wouldn't say. He just said he would come back later. Tall, dark, and handsome, built like a quarterback. And incredibly sexy, even with his five o'clock shadow."

Tanya glanced in Wade's direction, eyeing his bare chest appreciatively. "Yep, that's him."

"Lucky girl," Sandra commented enviously before ringing off.

"What did she say?" Wade asked after she had hung up the phone.

Tanya grinned mischievously. "That you're a hunk."

His face colored. "Oh."

"Why did you stop by the office yesterday?"

"I'd just heard Cliff had been killed, and I wanted to find out what he'd been working on for you. He'd hinted that it was something pretty big."

"You two discussed it, but he didn't give you any details?" She looked at him in surprise.

"Investigator-client relationship," he explained apologetically. "Cliff had a lot of integrity that way."

She nodded, accepting his explanation. "There's something else. Apparently, I was pretty upset about something before I left the office yesterday."

"Did Sandra say what it was?"

"No. I don't think she knew."

"Maybe you had a fight with someone at the office."

"Maybe." Tanya shrugged. "Maybe not. Maybe I'd just heard about Cliff. You said the explosion happened on the weekend, right?"

"Yeah. Sunday night."

"What was your brother-in-law doing at the office on a Sunday night?"

"According to my sister, Janie, Cliff's wife, he was working on some big case. Maybe it was yours. But back to Sandra. Why was she calling?"

"She said it was to see if I was okay. Oh, and to tell me some guy named Dave said it was okay if I took a few days off."

"Or maybe it was to check up on you, to find out if you're here." Wade's eyes narrowed. "I wonder. Could she be mixed up in this?"

"I have no idea. She seemed sincere enough on the phone."

"Jansen was right. We can't trust anyone until we get this thing figured out."

"I think Jansen was referring specifically to you," she responded dryly.

"True." He grinned. But then his smile faded as he added more seriously, "But Tanya, who else can you trust at the moment?"

His words hung ominously over the silence that followed, making her shiver. That was a very good question.

A knock sounded at the door.

Tanya and Wade glanced at each other.

"Now what?" he asked.

"Grand Central Station," she muttered as she made her way past him toward the door. "Who is it?"

"It's Martha, your neighbor. I have your cat."

"Okay. Hang on a second." She turned to Wade. "That explains the cat food I found in the kitchen."

She opened the door, and a generously proportioned, middle-aged woman breezed into the room, holding fast to a plump orange tabby. The cat meowed loudly at the sight of Tanya, and she instinctively held out her arms. Martha plunked the cat into them.

"Hi. Wasn't sure if you were home from the hospital yet, until I heard someone knocking on your door earlier. I found Charlie on my balcony, of all places. Poor guy must have jumped over after all the excitement the other day. Anyway, I kept him for you until you—." She broke off midsentence as she caught sight of Wade. "Oh my," she breathed, staring at his bare chest in admiration.

Martha gave Tanya a friendly elbow in the ribs. "Way to go, girlie."

"Thanks," Tanya smiled through gritted teeth. That elbow had hurt. "But if you'll please excuse us . . . "

"Oh. Of course. Of course, my dear. Gotta run. Nice meeting you, ah . . . ?"

"Wade Scott, ma'am."

"Nice meeting you, Wade Scott. You take care of Tanya, now, you hear?"

With a final wink at Tanya, Martha waltzed out into the hall. Tanya shut the door and turned back to Wade, a huge grin plastered across her face. "Oh my," she drawled, mimicking Martha's awestruck tone.

Wade gave her a disgusted look. "I think I'll put my shirt on," he muttered.

The cat meowed again and butted his head against Tanya's chin. She cuddled him closer, and he began to purr loudly. "Oh, my poor baby. Are you glad to be home?" she cooed.

Wade went to the bedroom to find his T-shirt, thinking that he would give one hell of a lot to be that cat right about now.

He found Tanya in the kitchen, ladling out a generous proportion of canned cat food for Charlie.

"No wonder that cat's so fat."

"He's not fat, Wade," she rebuked gently, reaching down to give Charlie a rub behind the ears. "He's a growing boy. He needs his calories."

"Yeah, but he's growing in the wrong direction."

She glanced at Wade in alarm. "Shhh! You'll hurt his feelings."

"Tanya, it's a cat," he started to argue back, before catching sight of the twinkle in her eyes. She set the plate of cat food down on the floor, and Charlie immediately dug in. "Coffee's ready. How do you take it?"

"Cream and sugar."

They sat down at the table and discussed what to do next. After rehashing the events of the past two days, they were forced to admit they had no clue where to begin.

"Well, we can't just sit here and wait for someone to strike again."

"I know, Tanya, but what else can we do?"

"Beats me," she sighed.

Charlie finished his breakfast and wandered over to rub his back against Tanya's leg.

"Poor Charlie. You must have had quite a scare the other day when Mommie fell off the balcony." She picked the cat up and kissed the top of its head. Charlie sat in her lap, purring contentedly as she fondled the fur under his chin.

"If only that cat could talk," Wade muttered. He was finding the present situation frustrating as hell. He didn't want to sit around any longer; he wanted to do something. It was like playing a game of cat and mouse. And he hated being the mouse.

She glanced at him sharply. "What did you say?"

"I was only joking, Tanya. Where's your sense of humor—." He broke off as he noticed the odd way she was staring down at Charlie so intently. "Tanya? What is it?"

She began to fumble with Charlie's flea collar. Removing it from his neck, she flipped it over in her hand. Her shout of triumph caused Charlie to leap from her lap and scramble out of the kitchen as fast as his four little legs could carry his big, tubby body.

"Look, Wade. Charlie *can* talk," she announced excitedly, holding out her hand. Attached to the inside of Charlie's collar was a tiny key.

"Well, I'll be damned. Thanks, Charlie."

"What do you suppose it belongs to?" she asked.

He took the collar from her hand and peeled the scotch tape from around the key. Holding it between his thumb and index finger, he studied it intently. "From the number engraved on it, I'd say it's some sort of locker key. Maybe from the bus or train depot."

"Then let's check it out!" Tanya was on her feet in an instant.

"No problem," he drawled, amused by her childlike exuberance. "But don't you think you should get dressed first?"

She made a face at him. "Of course. And I think I'll shower too. I won't be caught dead outside this apartment until I've washed my hair." Her mouth dropped as she realized Wade was privilege to her dishevelled state. "Oh my god, I must look hideous," she wailed.

"Good Lord, woman," he responded, voice laced with exasperation. His tone softened somewhat as she cringed. "Do you really think I care about that?"

She smiled weakly. "Sorry."

Tanya disappeared into the bathroom, closing the door behind her. A few minutes later, she opened the door again. "Wade!"

"What is it?" he called from the kitchen where he was rinsing out the coffee pot.

"Come here."

He set the glass pitcher on the counter and went to see what the problem was.

"How on earth am I going to wash my hair?"

That was a good question. The bandage across her forehead precluded putting her head under the water. He thought for a moment.

"Okay. Put your back against the edge of the tub and lean back. I'll wash it for you."

"What? You will not!"

"Got a better suggestion?"

She frowned. "No. Not really."

"Well, then. C'mon. Let's get this over with. Hand me the shampoo."

Resigned, she grabbed the plastic bottle and gave it to him. "Careful of my ribs."

"Don't worry, I haven't forgotten," he told her, and immediately wished he'd kept his mouth shut. He could see she was also thinking back to last night, when he had held her tenderly against him, careful not to further bruise her battered body as he made sweet love to it. The look on her face spoke volumes.

"Just wash my hair, Wade."

He leaned over her and turned on the water, taking a moment to adjust the temperature so as not to burn her scalp. "Okay. Put your head under."

He poured the soap into his hand and began to massage it into her scalp. He worked the lather through her hair, starting at the roots and moving his way down toward the tips. The slippery soap made her hair silky smooth to the touch, reminding him of the other parts of her body that he knew were equally as soft. He was finding the whole experience quite the turn on, much to his chagrin, and was sorely tempted to undo the belt around her dressing gown and rub other parts of her body just as dutifully.

The gentle touch of Wade's hands made Tanya think back to the way they had moved so expertly over her bare skin the previous evening, and she felt her body heat up at the memory. He'd been quite the skilled and tender lover, so careful not to hurt her yet determined to ensure she reached the height of ecstasy over and over again. It had certainly been a night to remember. The trouble was, those wonderful memories left her wanting more.

His hands began to rub her scalp in a gentle, circular pattern.

"Mmm, that feels nice," Tanya purred without thinking.

He glanced down at her, and their gaze met and locked. She saw the awareness and the desire in his eyes, could feel the sudden tension in his hands before he forced himself to relax once again. Though he never said a word, a silent conversation passed between them. It was a communication at the most basic, primal level.

The naked hunger in his eyes caused her breath to catch in her throat. Her heart began to pound harder and faster, and a slight tremor shook her body as a bolt of fiery heat snaked through it. Damn it, why had she come up with the stupid rule that they be business partners only?

She continued to stare up at him, unable to break eye contact. At that moment, she was his, and she knew he knew it. All he had to do was open the front of her dressing gown, and she would welcome him to her with open arms and eager anticipation.

He looked away first, focusing instead on the task at hand with grim determination.

She put a hand on his arm. "Wade?"

"Yes," he said through gritted teeth.

"Maybe when this is all over, we can kind of . . . start over?"

"Yeah, maybe," he grunted, knowing it to be impossible and yet wishing it were not the case.

He gave her hair a final rinse and turned off the water. After squeezing out as much moisture as he could, he grabbed a towel. "Okay, sit up."

She complied and used the towel to wrap her wet hair. "Thanks, Wade," she told him, relieved that her voice sounded almost normal.

"You're welcome." He stood up, and backed off a couple of steps. "Why don't I leave you to it," he added, and then high-tailed it out of there before he lost complete control of his senses.

Tanya closed the door and sat down on top of the toilet seat until she could get her body back under control, sorely tempted to chase after him and demand he take her to bed this very instant. Oh, how she wished her memory would return so she could deal with whoever was after her and then be free to chase after Wade herself. A tiny, self-satisfied smile curved her lips. She doubted he would be hard to catch.

She finished showering, dried her hair and added a touch of makeup to her still too pale complexion. Wade took his turn in the bathroom, and shortly after that, they were ready to leave.

Tanya paused at the door as Charlie ran up to them, meowing and pacing with agitation.

"What's wrong with your cat?"

"I'm not sure. Maybe he just doesn't want us to leave."

Charlie began pawing at the carpet.

"Oh, oh. You know, Wade, I don't remember seeing a litter box anywhere in the apartment."

Wade frowned. "Me neither." He looked at the cat thoughtfully. "You don't suppose he's toilet trained, do you?"

She laughed. "I somehow doubt it." She tapped her index finger on the edge of her chin. "Now, if I were me, where would I put the litter box?"

"Well, if it's not inside, then the only other possible place it can be is outside." He walked over toward the balcony and slid back the curtains. "Ah ha! What did I tell you?"

He slid open the doors and stepped outside. Then he laughed. "A kitty outhouse?" he chortled, referring to the name imprinted in the plastic cover over the litter box. "Now I've seen everything."

He brought the litter box in, and Charlie ran toward it gratefully, disappearing inside the hole to go about his business in private.

"So where do we try first?" she asked as they settled themselves into his truck.

"Bus or train depot? Take your pick."

She spotted some loose change in the bottom of the vehicle's coffee cup holder, and grabbed a quarter. She tossed it into air and caught it with one hand, slapping it on the top of the other. She lifted her hand. "Train station."

Wade nodded and pointed the truck in the proper direction.

"By the way, don't you have to go to work today? I assume you work for Able Construction," she added, referring to the name painted on both sides of his truck.

"The guys can make do without me for a few days. They're a good crew. I trust them to do a fair day's work even when the boss isn't around."

She looked at him in surprise. "You own the company?"

"It's a family business. My father started it."

"Oh. Well then, I suppose you can take as much time off as you want," she acknowledged.

It didn't take long to drive to the train station. Wade parked the truck, and they walked toward the main building. Inside, they were disappointed to find that the numbering system on the lockers there didn't match up with the key in Wade's pocket.

"Let's try the bus depot," he suggested.

"Okay."

He glanced at her face, noting the disappointment reflected there. "Don't worry. I have a feeling we'll be lucky next time around."

He was right. Tanya's heart quickened as she approached the panel of lockers numbered with sequence AB, the same as on the key. Her eyes flitted up and down the rows.

"Here it is."

Wade handed her the key.

"Cross your fingers," she told him, fitting the key inside the lock and turning it in a clockwise direction. "Success," she announced as the locking mechanism released.

The locker door swung open, and she retrieved a small package from inside, depositing it inside her shoulder bag.

"Let's get out of here," Wade suggested.

"Okay. We can open this in the truck."

They exited the building and walked quickly through the parking lot. Once Wade had pulled out into the street, Tanya took the brown envelope from her purse and ripped one end open.

"What's inside?" Wade asked, glancing over to get a look at the papers she was flipping through.

"Interesting. It's a bunch of photocopies of canceled checks drawn on Pacific Realtors' bank account. Large ones, and they're all made out to Starbright Enterprises."

Chapter Five

"I'm not sure this is such a good idea," Wade commented as he eyed the dark offices of Pacific Realtors a short way up the street.

Tanya shrugged her shoulders as she put on her gloves. "What choice do we have? Starbright Enterprises isn't listed in the phone book, and directory assistance has nothing on them. There has to be an address in the accounts payable files. Besides, I work here, remember. If we get caught, I'll just tell them I was coming in to pick up some work I wanted to do at home."

With a last, furtive glance around the area, she opened the truck door and jumped out. "C'mon Wade," she ordered and started across the street.

He raised his eyes skyward a moment before stepping out of the truck. It was just after midnight, and the street appeared deserted, but he was still nervous as hell. Break and enter was still break and enter, regardless of whether she had a key to the place. If they weren't careful, they would both end up in jail before the night was through.

He crossed the street and hurried up the sidewalk after her, hoping his truck would look as though it belonged where he had parked it beside the stockpile of cement at the construction site of another office tower. He hoped that the company name printed on his truck door would prevent any passing police cruiser from stopping to check out the abandoned vehicle. With any luck, the officer would assume that some employee had left the company truck there overnight and would be returning for it in the morning.

Tanya had already reached the top step of the main entrance by the time he managed to catch up with her, and was trying her third key in the lock.

"Got it," she crowed, just as he was about to ask if she had checked first to see if there was a security system on the premises.

A sudden shrill beeping cut loudly into the silence of the night, startling both of them.

"Damn, there *is* a security system installed. Let's get out of here quick." Wade was already halfway down the steps, and fully convinced that he was going to throttle her once they reached the safety of his truck.

"No problem." She opened the door and stepped up to the monitor, where she quickly keyed in a series of four digits. The beeping stopped, and an all-clear message flashed across the display.

Wade joined her inside. "You remembered the password."

"It appears that way," she commented with a casual shrug of her shoulders.

He raised an eyebrow at her suspiciously.

"Well, I wasn't exactly sure," she admitted, "but I decided to go with my instincts."

"Damn it, Tanya, you're too impulsive," he began, but she cut him off with a snort of disdain.

"Lighten up, Wade. I got us in, didn't I?"

He gave up. Not that he had much choice; she was already through the second set of doors and halfway down the hall, heading toward the back of the office.

They clicked on their flashlights. Wade kept his pointed toward the floor, but Tanya swung hers in every which direction as she examined the office set up. The white spot of light jumped from floor to ceiling to walls, spinning wildly around the room.

"Try to keep the light away from the windows," he cautioned, sighing inwardly with exasperation. She would make a terrible crook.

"Oh, okay. Good idea," she agreed with belated realisation. "I wonder where I sit. Or what I even do here." She approached a desk situated close to what looked like the executive offices. "Well, I'm not the secretary," she commented to Wade, holding up a picture frame containing a print of a man and woman in their early thirties surrounded by three young children, two cats, and a dog.

She shone her light over the remainder of the desk, crying out in triumph as her eye picked up a name at the top of the pile of *From the Desk of* note paper. "Hey, this is where Sandra sits."

"See if you can find your desk," he suggested. "Maybe we'll find something related to Starbright Enterprises in it."

As Wade began pulling open filing cabinet drawers, Tanya checked each of the several workstations situated around the room. None of them appeared to be hers. She moved on to the individual offices. The plaque on the wall by the door of the first one she came to read Dave Dayner.

"Hey, look. This office belongs to Dave Dayner. He must be the one who told Sandra I could take a few days off. I suppose he's probably the boss. His is definitely the biggest office."

"Forget about him for now. Don't waste too much time," he warned. "The longer we stay, the greater our chances of getting caught."

"Yeah. Whatever," she grumbled under her breath as she continued on to the next office. This one had her name on it.

"I'm in here," she called out as she entered the office. A business card holder filled with her cards sat on one corner of the desk. She picked one up. "I'm the office manager."

"That explains your access to the checks. See what else you can turn up."

"Hey, this is a pretty nice office. You should come check it out."

"No." Wade wasn't the least bit interested in a sightseeing tour; he wanted them to find what they had come for and then get the hell out of there while the getting was still good. He walked over to the last row of filing cabinets and shone his light down the front of them. They were individually labelled in ascending order of the alphabet. "I think I may have found what we're looking for," he announced, opening the drawer marked with the letter "S."

Shining his light inside, he quickly flipped through the files until he came to Starbright Enterprises. He pulled the file and opened it up. "Damn. It's a post office box. But at least it's local." He laid the open file on top the cabinet and retrieved a pen and notepad from the inside pocket of his jacket. After scribbling down the post box number, he returned the file to its proper resting place in the cabinet.

He walked over to Tanya's office. "Let's get out of here," he started to say, and then realized that he was addressing an empty room. Where the hell had she gone to now? "Tanya?"

"I'm in here," came a muffled voice from inside Dave Dayner's office.

"Don't touch anything," he warned, but the sound of breaking glass told him it was too late.

"Oops!"

"What happened?" Wade raced into the room to find Tanya eyeing the pieces of a broken water glass scattered across the carpet, an almost comical expression of guilt on her face.

"I knocked it off by accident," she apologized.

He sighed. "Let's pick up the glass and put it in the trash somewhere. Maybe Dave Dayner won't remember it was sitting there. Or maybe he'll just assume the cleaning crew picked it up."

He noted her woebegone expression and offered a small smile of encouragement. "Don't worry about it. We're wearing gloves, so there won't be any fingerprints. As long as no one checks the memory on the security system, they'll never know we were here. It's even possible that everyone uses the same entrance code, but I wouldn't want to bet my life on it."

"I'm sorry. I guess I kind of made a mess of things. No pun intended." She grinned.

"You really crack me up," he responded dryly, and she burst into laughter at his comeback.

Together they scooped up as much glass as they could, using their gloves to spread the smaller particles deep into the carpet. After depositing the glass in the trash can in the kitchen, they hurried back to the truck.

"Wow! That was exciting. What an adrenaline rush," she enthused as Wade fired the engine to life.

He glanced at her sideways. "You've got a warped sense of excitement. I hope you aren't expecting us to make a habit of this."

She stuck her tongue out at him. "C'mon, admit it. It was a little bit fun, wasn't it?"

He rolled his eyes, not bothering to respond.

"Let's not go home yet. I'm so wide awake, I'll never sleep. Why don't we go have a drink somewhere? The bars are open for a while longer, aren't they?"

He glanced at his watch. "Yes, but I'm not sure you should be drinking alcohol with your head injury. It might cause further damage."

"What harm can one little drink do?"

"Not much, I guess. Where do you want to go?"

She frowned. "I have absolutely no idea. You know, this amnesia thing is really beginning to get on my nerves."

"Sorry, I forgot. There's a spot not far from here I think you'd like. It's not usually that crowded, and so that odds of running into someone who might know you are pretty slim."

"Why wouldn't I want to run into someone who knows me?"

Oops. He shouldn't have been thinking out loud. He couldn't very well tell her his real concern was not so much someone knowing her as someone knowing that she would not normally be out with him. One innocent comment and his cover would be blown sky high in one nuclear explosion of Tanya's temper. There was also the possibility that seeing someone she knew well would cause a full restoration of her memory, which would also result in his budding friendship with her suffering the same fiery fate. "I just thought you might be embarrassed if you couldn't recognize them," he improvised.

"Oh. You have a point. I'm not really into dealing with that tonight."

He took her to an English style pub he sometimes frequented when he needed quiet time to himself. The atmosphere was cosy, the service friendly, and the man who played guitar for the patrons pleasant to listen to. The regular crowd was somewhat older, another reason why he believed it would be reasonably safe to bring her here.

They sat down at an empty table and Wade ordered them each a beer.

"Too bad we didn't get a street address for Starbright tonight," he commented after the waitress had left their table.

"Yeah. But I don't want to worry about it at the moment. Let's talk about something else."

"Like what?"

"You."

"Me? What about me?"

"Well, for starters . . . do you have a girlfriend."

He raised an eyebrow in surprise. "Interested?"

"No, of course not," she lied. "I was just wondering, because . . . well because of what we did the other night. It wouldn't be very nice if you had fooled around on someone, you know."

"You're right, it wouldn't. So fortunately no, I don't have a girlfriend."

"Tell me about yourself," she urged. "You're the only person I know right now, but I really don't know the first thing about you."

"There's not much to know. As I told you, I run the family business. It takes most of my time."

"So what do you do when you're not working?"

He shrugged. "The usual, I guess. Take in the odd movie, have a drink or two with the guys, fit in a workout here and there, play at being an uncle . . . " His expression softened as his voice trailed off.

"You like being an uncle."

"Yeah, I sure do. I'm looking forward to having children of my own someday."

"Are they Cliff's kids?"

"Yes, they are." The smile disappeared. "Right now my parents have them out of the country on a 'holiday' until we figure it's safe for them to return. Janie couldn't go—she's actually in jail right now," he confided. "She wanted me to put up the bail, but I convinced her it was safer for her to stay where she was. She's not too happy about it, but she's agreed to do as I suggested."

"Why is your sister in jail?"

"After Cliff was killed, the police raided their house on an anonymous tip. They found a huge stash of cocaine—planted, of course. Then it was discovered that a large sum of money had been deposited recently in their bank account. Because it was a joint account, the police are accusing her of being involved. Someone has gone to a lot of time, trouble, and expense to make Cliff's death look like something other than it was, and I swore an oath to Janie I would do everything in my power to clear both of them."

"It sounds like whoever it was is pretty dangerous, Wade. If you're not careful, you could get seriously hurt. You might even end up like your brother-in-law."

"It's a risk I'll have to take. My sister needs me. And I won't have my nephews growing up believing their father was a criminal." He reached forward and took her hand. "I'm worried about you, too, Tanya," he told her, squeezing her fingers gently. "At least one and quite probably two attempts have been made on your life already. I want you to know that I'm going to do whatever I can to keep you out of harm's way."

A shiver of foreboding slithered down Tanya's spine. She could see he was entirely convinced that the fall from her apartment balcony was no accident, and that the mystery man in her hospital room had had more than just an idle chat on his mind. Until now, she'd been reassuring herself these events were all part of some simple misunderstanding that would sort itself out eventually, and then she and Wade would have a good chuckle over everything. But Wade was making it very clear with his chilling words and ominous expression that her present situation was no laughing matter.

A heavy weight pressed itself against her heart and lungs, and she fought a growing sense of panic. "Let's play pool," she suggested brightly, desperate for some sort of distraction from the icy fingers of fear which were slowly and insidiously tightening their grip on her inner organs.

"Do you play?" he asked, surprised at the suddenness of her request.

"There's only one way to find out," she announced, rising to her feet. "C'mon."

As it turned out, she strongly suspected she'd never even picked up a pool cue before. Wade was a good sport, however, showing her how to position the cue to shoot straight and coaching her on how to determine where to hit each ball in order to sink it. She was so bad that at one point, he put his arms around her and guided her shot with his hands. That had been a mistake, for the feathery touch of his warm breath on her cheek and the wonderful feel of his hard body pressed against hers had so distracted her that after that she'd been completely useless with the pool cue.

Shortly afterward, she laughingly agreed to give it up, and they finished their beers and left.

There was a brief awkward moment between them back at her apartment when it came time to say good night. Wade came to the rescue by walking over to her linen closet and pulling out one of the blankets he'd helped her fold and put away the previous afternoon.

"See you in the morning," he called back over his shoulder as he walked toward the couch in the living room.

She sighed heavily as she entered the bathroom to get ready for bed. Wade seemed not to mind in the least that he was sleeping alone tonight. Why, he had barely even hesitated before helping himself to her extra blankets. She wasn't sure whether to feel relieved or insulted.

"It's your own fault," she mumbled into the towel as she dried her face off. She had, after all, been the one to lay out the ground rules between them this morning. Strictly business, she'd told him then. And under the circumstances, it was best things remained that way, she told herself now.

What did Starbright Enterprises have to do with Cliff's death? she wondered as she drew back the covers. Why had she gone to the trouble of hiding copies of the canceled checks in a bus depot locker and then placing the key to the locker in Charlie's collar? Did whoever was after her know about the key to the locker? Was that what they were searching for when they broke into her apartment and trashed the place? She was so tired it hurt to think, but the questions kept coming, one right after the other.

A wave of bone-aching weariness overcame her as she snuggled herself down underneath the covers, and despite the questions spinning around and around inside her head, she fell asleep within moments of her head hitting the pillow.

* * * * *

She was standing outside on her balcony, looking down toward the ground. Suddenly the earth opened up to reveal a deep, yawning pit of black nothingness. She peered into its inky depths but could see no bottom surface, no end to the empty void expanding down into forever beneath her.

She became aware of a little girl standing beside her who was also staring down into the gaping hole.

"No! Oh, please don't go away," the little girl sobbed. "Please don't leave me."

Instinctively, Tanya reached out to comfort her, but the child would not be consoled. "It's not fair," she shouted at Tanya accusingly. "It's just not fair..."

* * * * *

Tanya woke, her face wet with tears. The dream had been strangely upsetting and oddly familiar, as if she'd been there before. Or perhaps she had dreamed it on another occasion. She frowned, thinking back to her nightmare of the previous evening. The exact details of it still remained a mystery, but she sensed that this dream and that nightmare were in fact related in some way.

The smell of freshly brewed coffee and the sound of bacon sizzling away in the frying pan interrupted her train of thought, and she stretched luxuriously, deciding that she could very quickly get used to sharing her apartment with her temporary roommate. Though of course she couldn't be certain, she sensed it had been a very long time since someone else had cooked her breakfast.

She pushed back the covers and reached for her dressing gown, her gurgling stomach informing her that yes, it was in fact time to eat. After taking a brief moment to brush her hair and splash her face with cool water, she joined Wade in the kitchen.

"Good morning, sleepyhead," he teased.

She glanced at the clock, surprised to see it was just after nine o'clock. Their late night espionage mission was no doubt responsible for her extended sleep in.

"Have a seat. Breakfast is ready."

She sat down obediently, and he brought her over a cup of coffee and a plate of bacon and eggs.

"Thanks Wade. This is a real treat."

He settled into a chair himself, and they chatted about inconsequential things over breakfast. But once they had finished eating, Wade poured them both a second cup of coffee, and their talk turned to more serious matters.

"So aside from staking out the post office, what else can we do now?"

"I don't know." Wade stood up and began to pace around the room, his frustration evident in each agitated step. It seemed no matter which way he turned, he stumbled right into another brick wall. First, it was Tanya's amnesia, and now their one lucky break had turned into what appeared to be yet another dead end. "I don't suppose we can convince anyone at the post office to give us any information about who owns post box number 1020."

"We could always break into the post office tonight and steal the information," Tanya offered brightly.

He gave her a speaking look. "Don't even think about it."

She shrugged indifferently, fighting to suppress the tiny smile tugging at the corner of her mouth. "Just trying to be helpful."

He sat down again with a tired sigh and rubbed the back of his neck with one hand. "Can I see the checks again?"

"Sure." She got up and retrieved the checks from her purse.

He glanced through the photocopied pages again, not really expecting to find anything new. Something on the reverse side of one of the checks caught his attention, however, and he looked a little closer. The stamp was faint, but the name of the bank which had accepted the deposit was Wells Fargo, the same bank he dealt with. The glimmerings of an idea began to form.

"Thanks." He handed the photocopies back to Tanya and stood up. "I'm going to take a shower, if you don't mind." He needed a chance to think things through. His brain felt rather sluggish this morning, and he was hoping a hot shower would revive him somewhat.

The steaming water cascading down over his body did just that, and Wade turned his face into it gratefully, feeling his mind slowly come awake. He thought through his idea carefully, and after a few minutes of careful deliberation, he felt reasonably confident it would work.

He picked up Tanya's pink razor from the edge of the tub where he'd left it yesterday, wishing he had something other than face soap for lubricant. He should really change his clothing as well, but that would mean going home, and he hesitated to bring Tanya with him. It was possible a visit to his house might jog her memory, and he was loathe to risk it. So short of leaving her on her own, which he did not want to do, he was stuck with what he was wearing.

He wondered if Tanya thought it strange he hadn't gone home to change his clothes. But perhaps she suspected she wasn't likely to get a straight answer if she were to question him about it. He knew she hadn't believed his explanation about why he'd omitted to tell her that Cliff was his brother-in-law. Not that he blamed her. It was pretty flimsy, and Tanya was not a stupid woman.

Nor was she one who normally let others take charge of her life. Yet even after finding out he had withheld information about Cliff, she'd let him stay. And it had not taken much effort on his part to talk her into it. All this was very much out of character for her. No doubt she had her own agenda, which she would reveal in her own good time.

On the other hand, it must be pretty terrifying not to know who she was or remember any details about her life prior to Tuesday morning. Perhaps she was tolerating him simply because it was preferable to being all alone in a world where nothing was familiar, no one was recognizable, and everyone was a potential adversary. Including him. Did she still secretly wonder which side he was on?

Twinges of guilt needled at him, for he couldn't honestly claim to be on her side. He had his own agenda to worry about, and he couldn't be entirely sure that it would not at some point conflict with hers. Still, as long as their needs remained in harmony, he would do everything he could to help her. And as long as he was around, no one was going to hurt her.

Except him, that is. How was she going to feel when she learned she had slept with the enemy? How could he have been such a cad? She would never forgive him when she found out, and it would make little difference to her pain and embarrassment that he wasn't going to be able to forgive himself either. Somehow, some way, he was going to make it up to her. It was the only way he would ever be able to look himself in the mirror again.

His troubled thoughts turned to bittersweet memories of what it had been like making love with Tanya Riverton. He'd experienced nothing like it with any other woman, and remembering the magic they'd made together while knowing he could never touch her again was causing him physical pain. It would have been much easier if he'd restrained himself the other night. At least then he could have lived out the rest his life never knowing what he would now be missing. He glanced down at his lower body, and then with a muttered curse switched off the hot water faucet.

Tanya sat at the kitchen table, sipping another cup of coffee as she fondled absently with Charlie's fur. Charlie's motor buzzed loud and strong as he remained happily oblivious to the silent debate taking place in the mind of his mistress. Nor did he appear particularly concerned that it had been running almost non-stop for the past forty-eight hours.

"What do you think he's really doing here, Charlie?" she asked her feline companion.

Charlie continued to purr happily, offering no answer to the number one question which had been nagging at Tanya since yesterday morning. Everything Wade had told her so far made sense, except for one thing. Not for a moment did she buy into his explanation for neglecting to mention his family connection to Cliff Peterson.

So then what *was* he doing here? She could only assume that he was looking for whatever information was lost somewhere inside her head. But for what purpose? On the one hand, he had sounded so sincere last night when speaking of his promise to help his sister, but she still had no idea why he hadn't told her about Cliff being his brother-in-law until Detective Jansen had let the cat out of the bag. Why had he kept the relationship a secret? Was it because, as the detective had intimated, he was involved in some sort of drug ring, and he needed some important information from her before he could complete his deal?

Though she found the idea a little hard to believe, she couldn't afford to discount any possibility at this point. Even so, when she took into consideration his words and actions over the past couple of days, the odds did appear remote. Nothing in the manner in which he had treated her was consistent with the type of behavior she would associate with a criminal mentality.

He'd been kind and considerate, helping her clean up the mess in her apartment, making sure he did most of the heavy lifting. He'd helped her wash her hair, done the dishes while she showered yesterday, and even made her breakfast this morning. His taking the initiative to change the locks on her apartment door had demonstrated genuine concern for her safety. And what about the way he'd ordered her to remain outside her apartment until he determined it was safe for her to enter? Or his promise last night that as long as he was there to protect her, no harm would befall her?

With her memory gone, instinct and intuition were all she had to rely on, and deep in her heart, she truly believed he was one of the good guys. Besides, she was starting to really like him. A lot. It was more than just physical attraction, although there was certainly plenty of that as well.

That body of his was something else. Lean and solid from years of physical labor, his muscular frame would be the envy of most body builders, for there was a hard strength about him that couldn't be developed simply by lifting weights. It added a sense of power to his presence and an air of sexy toughness. Yet the way he'd made love to her had been so gentle, and his touch so soft and delicate that she could have cried at the beauty of it.

There was so much about him she admired. Like his calm and rational approach to situations, unlike her tendency to jump in with both feet and no thought for the consequences. The patient way in which he'd dealt with her rudeness and deliberate baiting back at the motel. The speed at which he'd been at her side after her nightmare, offering comfort with warm and caring concern. And after that, he'd remained a gentleman to the very end, offering her one final chance to say no, even though she could tell he'd been hovering perilously close to the point of no return.

Though he'd been very much aroused, he had loved her slowly and thoroughly, taking every care to satisfy her completely before looking after his own need. Afterward, he had studied her in awe as if he'd been just as moved by the experience as she, and finding it equally hard to believe that making love could be so incredibly fabulous between a man and a woman.

All in all, he was a pretty incredible guy. So why then had she insisted on an arm's length business relationship between the two of them? Had her sudden loss of memory also rendered her temporarily insane?

She grinned conspiratorially at the cat on her lap. "Well, Charlie, it *is* a woman's prerogative to change her mind."

She was still smiling to herself when Wade returned to the kitchen.

"You're looking pretty pleased with yourself at the moment."

Tanya started, so engrossed in her thoughts that she'd missed hearing him come into the room. She glanced up, appreciating again both his muscular physique and his masculine good looks. Though his appearance was softened somewhat by damp curls glistening in the sunlight and a rosy, after-the-shower glow in his cheeks, he was still very deliciously all male. Every solid, brawny, sensational inch of him. She noted a fresh light in his eyes and a jaunty spring in his step that hadn't been present earlier this morning. It appeared he was rather happy about something himself.

"So are you," she told him.

"As a matter of fact, I am. I have a plan. And, Tanya"—he grinned—"you're going to be perfect for the part."

Chapter Six

"Wade! It's great to see you. Come on in." Don Cummings stood in the doorway of his office, smiling broadly as Wade and Tanya rose from the couch in the waiting area and walked toward him. He eyed Tanya with undisguised curiosity as they drew near.

"Hi Don." Wade extended his hand in greeting. "I'd like you to meet Tanya Riverton," he added once the two men had shaken hands. "Tanya, this is Don, my friendly neighborhood bank manager."

"Hi Tanya. Nice to meet you."

"Nice to meet you too, Don." She noticed that he was staring at her forehead. "Please excuse the bandage. I fell the other day and gave myself a bit of a bump. Nothing serious," she assured him with a self-deprecating laugh.

"Glad to hear it," Don responded with a friendly smile. "Why don't you two have a seat and tell me what I can do for you today," he suggested, waving them toward the two empty chairs sitting in front of his desk.

The three of them sat down.

"I was hoping you could give me a bit of information about a customer from your downtown Seattle branch that's asked me to do some work for them. I know the rules about client privacy," he assured Don before the man could voice his forthcoming objection, "but Sandy is on holidays this week, and these guys are in a hurry for me to get started. I'd sure hate to lose the business simply because I couldn't confirm their credit rating in time. Couldn't you just pull them up on your screen and let me know if they have a positive bank balance or at least a decent line of credit available to them?"

Don was silent as he considered the request. "I'm really not supposed to do this you know . . . but I suppose it wouldn't hurt to give you that small bit of information," he conceded after a moment's thought on the matter. "What's the company name?"

"Starbright Enterprises," Wade answered.

Tanya stood up and moved toward the credenza against the side wall. "What a lovely collection," she exclaimed, referring to the group of model ships on display. "Do you mind if I take a closer look?"

"Go ahead," Don told her as he punched Starbright's name into his keyboard. "The collection was started by my grandfather, who was a merchant mariner during the war. Both my father and I have added to it over the years," he explained as he waited for the computer to retrieve the name. "Okay, I've got the account number. Just give me a minute to pull up the info."

He pressed a few more keys. "All right, here it is. Everything looks—," he began, but Tanya's sharp cry stopped him midsentence.

Wade leaped to his feet and was at her side in an instant. Don followed close behind. Tanya clung to Wade's arm, moaning pitifully.

"What's wrong?" Don asked, his brow creased with alarm.

"I have to sit down," she gasped. "Wade, help me. I'm so dizzy."

She reached out and grasped the edge of Don's desk, and then stumbled around behind it to fall down into the chair he had just vacated. She put her face down on the desk. "I'll be all right in a moment," she groaned.

"Don, is everything all right?" asked a concerned voice from the doorway.

"Water," Tanya gasped.

"Could she have some water?" Wade asked.

"Mary, please bring us a glass of water," Don instructed his secretary. "Should I call for an ambulance?" he asked Wade nervously.

"That won't be necessary," Tanya told him in a weak voice. "I'm starting to feel better already. I think I may have stood up too quickly earlier."

"It's her—."

"I'm pregnant, you see," she interjected before Wade could finish.

What? Wade almost shouted it aloud, such was his surprise.

That hadn't been part of the plan! Trust Tanya to improvise with something like that just to throw him off balance. Then another thought stunned him. After the other night, she very well could be! The concept was so mind-boggling, he completely missed Don's next words.

"Wade, darling, Don just congratulated you," Tanya's voice cut through the thick fog of panic which had temporarily shut down his brain.

"What?" He stared at her blankly.

She rolled her eyes skyward before turning back to Don. "Don't mind Wade, Don. We've only just found out, and he's having trouble taking it all in." She grabbed Wade's arm and looked up at him adoringly. "We're so happy. Aren't we, darling?"

"Ecstatic," he confirmed, glancing down at her with a private look that told her exactly what he was feeling.

"Congratulations," Don repeated and offered his hand. Wade shook it, feeling a little silly.

"Wade, darling, can this business with this Starlight or Starflite or whatever company wait until later? I really would like you to take me home, if you don't mind."

"Of course, darling." He helped her to her feet, placing a supportive arm around her shoulders. "Are you sure you'll be all right?" he asked solicitously. "Should I carry you to the truck?"

She smiled sweetly as she caught his sarcasm, and only Wade was privilege to the mischievous twinkle in her eye. "No, sweetheart, it's okay. I'm sure I'll make it."

"I'll call you later, Don," he tossed back over his shoulder as they exited the office.

"For Pete's sake, Tanya," he started as soon as they were outside the bank. "That wasn't part of the plan. Warn me next time you're going to improvise, will you?"

"Well, it worked, didn't it?"

"You got it?"

"Four two zero South Hinds Street," she announced triumphantly.

"Good girl." He grinned. "I forgive you for almost giving me a heart attack in there."

"I knew that big, strong body of yours would stand the shock," she responded with a heartless shrug that didn't quite jive with the laughter dancing in her eyes. "Now c'mon, let's check out Starbright Enterprises."

"Okay, we'll drive by and take a look. But that's it for now," he warned, "until we know exactly who and what we're dealing with. Right now the only advantage we have is the element of surprise."

She opened her mouth to disagree but then closed it again, honesty forcing to her to acknowledge the soundness of his argument. Marching through the front door and demanding to know what the hell was going on, though tempting, wouldn't accomplish anything other than to warn the bad guys that she and Wade were onto them.

"Okay," she sighed. "You're right, of course. Patience just isn't one of my many virtues. But I did okay in Don's office, didn't I?" she added, brightening a little. "Did you notice how I waited for exactly the right moment to glance toward the screen, making it look like the most natural movement in the world. The poor man didn't suspect a thing. Maybe I should have been an actress."

"Yes, but don't forget who coached you." He grinned back.

She stuck her tongue out at him as they climbed into the truck. Wade took a moment to punch the address into the GPS navigation screen on his dash and review the recommended route before pulling out of the bank's parking lot and working his way toward the I-90. Tanya continued to prattle on enthusiastically about her Oscar-winning performance, and it was some time before she finally noticed Wade wasn't really paying attention.

"What is it, Wade?" she asked, noting his concerned expression.

"I think we're being followed. Don't turn around," he added quickly, as she started to look back over her shoulder.

"What are you going to do?"

Wade changed lanes and merged onto the I-405 southbound ramp.

"This isn't the right direction. Where are we going?"

"You're going shopping," he replied, nodding toward Factoria Mall on the left.

"What are you talking about?"

"You're going shopping," Wade repeated patiently as he took the Coal Creek Parkway exit. "At Factoria Mall."

"What? You want me to go shopping at a time like this? Are you nuts?" she demanded.

"Slow down a minute. You're the decoy. I follow whoever follows you," he explained patiently. "Okay?"

"Oh . . . okay. But you'll be close behind me, right?" she asked nervously. It was easy enough to be impulsive and daring with her companion's muscle-bound body there to protect her, but the thought of wandering through a shopping mall all alone with some unknown stranger stalking her was a little scary. She realized this would be the first time Wade had left her side since she woke up in the motel room.

Wade entered the north end of the mall near the Safeway and pulled into a parking spot not far from the entrance to the main section of the mall, "Of course," he answered, placing his hand on her shoulder and giving it a gentle squeeze of reassurance. "Remember what I told you last night, Tanya. No one, and I mean no one, is going to hurt you while I'm around."

She gave him a small, hesitant smile. "I know. I know. It's just that . . . Oh, what the hell. Let's get this over with, shall we?"

Wade cut the engine, and they both stepped out of the truck. Together, they strolled toward the mall entrance as nonchalantly as possible.

"Give me a kiss just outside the doors to make it look like we're going to split up once we get inside," he instructed as they approached the building. We'll go in together, and then I'm going to duck out of sight. Walk slowly toward Old Navy, and then up to Target at the far end of the mall. Take your time and poke around in front of a few stores, but stay out in the open where I can see you," he cautioned.

"Okay."

He picked up on the slight quiver in her tone. "Don't worry," he told her again, squeezing her hand for added reassurance. "Everything is going to work out fine. Once you get to the far end, turn around and work your way back down the other side. When I meet up with you, ask me if I got everything I needed, and once I agree with you, we'll leave. If I say no, that means I wasn't able to get a good enough look at the guy, and we'll have to think of another way to flush him out."

She nodded her agreement, not quite trusting herself to speak. The sane part of her was somewhat nervous about the venture she was about to embark upon, yet the adventurous part was responding to the thrill of the adrenaline rushing through her veins and eagerly anticipating the challenge of playing cat and mouse with a possible killer. The two warring factions within were playing havoc with her insides; no doubt her nerves would be completely shot after today. Thank goodness she would have Wade's calm strength to lean on once this little escapade was over.

Glancing at her companion, she again questioned her sanity. She barely knew the man, yet she was willing to place her life in his hands by doing as he said without question. He could be anyone, even her own worst enemy, for all she knew, and yet for some unknown, inexplicable reason she trusted him with an unwavering faith like she knew she could no other. She would do exactly as he said, not because she was brave of heart or inherently suicidal, but because she knew deep in her heart of hearts that he would not let her down.

They reached the main entrance, kissed and stepped inside the doors. Another brief squeeze of encouragement from Wade's hand, and she was on her own.

Breathing slowly to calm her jittery stomach and help relax her stiff shoulders and neck, she sauntered casually toward the first clothing store on her right, somehow resisting the tantalizing urge to glance back over her shoulder. She pawed through a sales rack in the doorway, noting her trembling fingers with almost clinical detachment. Realising she had no idea what she was looking at, she moved to the display window next door and pretended to concentrate on the latest fashions inside it.

The minutes ticked by, and her sense of blind helplessness intensified with each passing second. The not knowing if or how close behind her some evil stranger was stalking was playing on her nerves, stretching them to the point where she felt ready to snap. The tension played tricks with her mind, transforming her foe into a giant, green-eyed monster and screaming out that it was right behind her, ready to pounce. She could almost feel the sharp points of its teeth pricking into the back of her spine.

Tanya forced herself to move slowly, though every inch of her longed to race around the mall at breakneck speed and throw herself into the safe haven of Wade's arms. So what if Wade was disgusted by her lack of courage? At this particular moment, she was too frightened to care.

She reached the far end of the mall, and turned around to begin the final stretch of her journey back to the safe haven of Wade's reassuring smile. Just as she was starting to relax with the knowledge that she was going to make it back in one piece, the prickling at the base of her neck suddenly intensified. Before she realized what was happening, a strong arm grabbed her from behind and spun her through a set of doors and into the hallway leading to the public washrooms. A quick glance down the hallway showed there was no one in sight. A firm hand clamped down over her mouth. Survival instinct took over, and immediately she bit down on it as hard as she could.

Her assailant removed his hand, cursing violently.

"Wade!" she screamed at the top of her lungs, knowing full well that the heavy doors were effectively blocking the sound of her voice and that there was no possible way Wade could hear her. She was on her own. Sheer panic overcame her, and she struck out blindly, gnashing her teeth and kicking her legs until her attacker pressed one of his legs against both of her thighs and a forearm against her neck, effectively immobilizing her. The pressure of his arm choked off the supply of oxygen to her brain, and she began to feel the effects immediately, finding it difficult to think clearly and impossible to call out for help.

"Cut it out, you dumb bitch," an angry male voice whispered.

The doors burst open wide, and Wade tackled the man with his legendary quarterback hold. The two of them hit the cement tiles, and Wade was on his opponent in an instant, clenched fist up by his ear and ready to strike. He heard Tanya scream again, and felt the cold barrel of a gun press against his right temple.

Wade froze on the spot, and the man beneath him pushed himself free and scrambled to his feet. He barely had time to straighten his jacket before the doors opened again, and several concerned male bodies poked their faces inside.

"Hey! He's got a gun," one of the men shouted, and the doors slammed shut again. "SECURITY!" they heard him screech at the top of his lungs.

"Damn." The man with the gun swore softly. "Get up," he motioned to Wade with the barrel of his gun. "Against the wall." Wade climbed to his feet, his palms open in front of him non-aggressively. He moved to stand beside Tanya, who immediately latched onto him with both hands and buried her face in his chest. She began to sob quietly, and he instinctively put one arm around her shoulders in comfort.

"You can't shoot us in cold blood," he told the two strangers in the most reasonable tone he could manage. "There are too many witnesses outside."

A commanding voice from outside the doors confirmed the truth of Wade's statement. "Mall Security. Put your gun away, come out with your hands up, and no one gets hurt."

The two men looked at each other. An unspoken conversation passed between them, and man Wade had knocked down nodded his agreement to something.

"Relax officer," the man with the gun called out. "We're FBI agents. Hold your fire while I slide my badge under the door."

Tanya glanced up at Wade. "FBI?" she mouthed silently, the unspoken question burning in her eyes. Wade shrugged, equally as confused.

There was a short silence while the security officer examined the badge. After a few moments it came back through under the door.

"You have my full support, Agent Turvey," the security officer advised him. "How can I help you, sir?"

"Get those people away from the door, and tell them to go about their business. Then show us to your office so we can speak to these people here in private."

"Sure thing, sir. Just give me a minute here."

The four of them stared at each other in silence as they listened to the mall's security officer thanking the crowd outside for their help and advising them that everything was now under control. A million questions spun around in Tanya's head until she couldn't remain silent another moment longer.

"Why is the FBI spying on us?" she demanded.

The man with the badge holstered his gun with a sigh. "We weren't spying on you," he told her.

"You were following us around," she challenged. "What's the difference?"

Wade silently applauded her defiant tone, admiring her gutsy attitude. "You two have got some serious explaining to do," he added, cold anger lending a hard edge to his words.

"We want to talk to you about Cliff Peterson's death," Agent Turvey explained.

"Then why not just knock on my door in a civilized fashion, instead of holding a gun to Wade's head like some murderous maniac?"

"We think someone is watching you very closely, Ms. Riverton. We didn't want to risk your safety by alerting them to the fact that you've spoken with the FBI. Of course, that's no longer possible after the stunt your friend just pulled," he added, tossing a disgusted look in Wade's direction.

"How was he supposed to know the guy who grabbed me was an FBI agent? You should be thankful I have him to protect me from idiots like your friend here who almost gave me a heart attack. Why the hell didn't he tell me who he was?"

"I was just about to introduce myself to you, when you bit me," the other man accused.

"Oh! Did I hurt you?" she asked, her voice laced with sweet concern.

"Yeah," he admitted.

"Good!" she snapped back, her eyes flashing angrily.

"All right, Ms. Riverton," Turvey interrupted in a soothing tone. "I understand you were given a scare, but please understand we thought our way was for the best. We're all on the same side here."

A knock on the doors interrupted them. "All clear, Agent Turvey. Would you like to follow me to the security office?"

"We'll be right out," Turvey called back. He turned back to Wade and Tanya. "Okay. We'll follow the security guard to his office. I'll go in front, and Davis here will cover our backs, just in case."

"Just in case what?"

"In my line of work, you never know, Ms. Riverton."

Tanya glanced at Wade, her eyebrows raised in askance.

"Better do as he says," Wade whispered when she seemed about to protest. "And stick close to me."

She hugged him briefly, a silent thanks for being there for her. He smiled back reassuringly.

Turvey opened the doors, and Wade and Tanya followed him out into the mall. Wade placed his arm firmly around Tanya and gently urged her along. She moved beside him obediently, her body still in shock from the surprise assault and subsequent chain of events and her mind clinging with childlike faith to the belief that Wade would keep her safe.

The group walked quickly and with purpose toward the mall security office, the men examining the crowd with guarded glances, all three alert for possible danger. There were a few curious passersby, but they quickly turned away at Wade's hard stare.

Once inside the office, Agent Turvey took charge, thanking the security guard and closing the door behind him. "Why don't we all sit down and start over," he suggested.

Wade helped Tanya into a chair and sat down beside her. "You first," he ordered.

"All right. Cliff Peterson called us the day he died to tell us he had come across something we should know about while doing some investigative work for a Ms. Tanya Riverton. He died before we could get the details."

"That's it?" Tanya demanded. "That's all you know?"

"I'm afraid so, Ms. Riverton. We were hoping you could tell us what this was all about."

"Sorry, no can do. I've got amnesia."

"So we heard. We also heard you 'fell' from your apartment balcony the day after Cliff Peterson died, and then you were attacked in the hospital. Are you *sure* there's not anything you can tell us? Anything at all? You never know. Something which seems insignificant to you might mean something to us."

"Well," she began, stopping as she felt the pressure of Wade's foot as it bumped against hers. "No, can't think of anything, Agent Turvey," she continued after a moment. "Sorry."

The agent frowned.

"Are you sure?" his partner persisted.

"If the lady says she's sure, then she's sure, Davis," Wade growled.

Davis stared at him. *I won't forget what happened earlier*, his eyes seemed to say.

I won't either, Wade glared back.

Turvey sighed. "Well, that's it, then." He stood up, indicating the interview was over. "I suggest you go home and stay put until we figure out what's going on."

"I beg your pardon?" Wade couldn't believe his ears. "You want her to wait in her apartment like a sitting duck? Why doesn't she paint a bull's eye on her forehead for good measure? After all this, I think she needs some protection. Starting now, with you guys."

"I really don't think that will be necessary, Scott," Davis told him in a condescending manner. "We'll take care of things."

Wade stood up, pulling Tanya with him. "C'mon, let's get out of here, Tanya," he instructed, eyeing both men in disgust.

She followed him back out through the mall.

"Why didn't you want me to tell them about Starbright Enterprises?" she demanded once they were out of earshot.

"Maybe it's normal to distrust a guy who holds a gun to your head, but I have a feeling they're not telling us everything they know."

"But Wade, they don't have to. They're the FBI."

"Yeah. But it's your life they're messing with."

"And yours," she acknowledged quietly. "So what do we do now?"

"Be vewy, vewy careful," he told her, imitating Elmer Fudd's cartoon voice with a wicked grin.

She laughed, his sense of humor restoring hers. "Those guys were rather stuffy, weren't they? Do you think Agent Davis will hold a grudge?"

"Oh, yeah," he drawled, remembering the hate stare the man had given him in the security office. Davis had been itching for a piece of him, and the feeling was definitely mutual. The memory of Davis holding Tanya pinned helplessly against the wall returned, charging him with renewed anger all over again. "And so will I," he added darkly.

They stepped outside the mall. It was quickly moving toward midafternoon, and the sun was beginning to cast long shadows on the vehicles in the parking lot. Wade estimated they would have just enough time to drive by Starbright Enterprises before the evening rush hour began in earnest.

"What now?" Tanya repeated her earlier question.

"If we hurry, we can still make it to South Hinds Street before the traffic gets too heavy. I don't want to risk it during rush hour."

"Why not?"

"If we get stuck in a traffic jam in front of Starbright, we might be recognized by someone coming out of the building."

Lord almighty, Tanya thought in exasperation. Was there any possible consequence he would not consider?

"Then you would just have to kill them," she shrugged, and then sighed at the shocked look on his face. "I'm just kidding, Wade. You know, sometimes you're just a little too serious for your own good."

He stopped dead in his tracks and stared down at her, his shocked expression changing to one of annoyance. "For my own good? What about yours? Someone out there is trying to hurt you. Maybe even kill you. Don't you think you should be taking things a little more seriously?" he growled.

She lowered her head in shame. "I'm sorry, Wade. You're right." She sought his eyes once more. "You're absolutely right," she repeated, her pained expression begging him to understand. "It's the stress, I guess. I have to let it out somehow. I'm sorry I'm taking it out on you."

The anger drained out of him as quickly as it came, replaced by tender compassion for her obvious distress over the way her words had hurt him, and instant forgiveness for the slip of her sharp tongue. He knew she hadn't really meant it.

"It's all right. I understand. Come here," he ordered softly, opening his arms.

She stepped into the inner circle of his embrace, but the reassuring heat from his body did little to dispel the cold shadow of dread which had suddenly enveloped her, despite the warmth of the sun's rays on her back. A sudden bolt of fear turned her blood to ice, and an overwhelming feeling of impending doom gripped her heart in its icy clutches.

"I'm afraid, Wade. The FBI doesn't waste its time getting mixed up with small-time stuff, and I'm sure Cliff wouldn't have called them unnecessarily. I don't know what I've dragged you into, but I hope it doesn't get us both killed."

He felt her tremble and kissed the top of her head. "Don't worry. Nothing's going to happen to either one of us."

"I just have this awful feeling," she began, and then whimpered in fear as he stiffened suddenly.

"Oh, oh."

"What is it?"

"That cart of groceries is going to ram my truck."

Tanya lifted her head and saw the runaway buggy heading toward his truck, which was still quite a way from where they were standing. She could see it was going to make one heck of a dent in the side of his vehicle.

"Oh, no," she gasped.

"Don't worry," he laughed suddenly. "It's just a truck."

They watched as the cart collided with the truck, which instantly exploded into a mass of brilliant flames.

Chapter Seven

Tanya barely had time to register what was happening before Wade pushed her to the ground and covered her body with his. As the sound of the initial explosion died in her ears, she could hear the tinkling of glass shards striking the vehicles all around them. A secondary blast erupted, sending a chunk of twisted metal spinning into the front window of the vehicle next to them. It shattered into a million pieces, several hundred of them spraying down onto the pavement beside them and across the back of Wade's leather jacket. Then there was a brief, dead silence, and the nightmare was over as quickly as it began, save for the vicious crackle of flames as they devoured the last of the vehicle.

General chaos erupted around them. Footsteps thundered past as concerned citizens rushed to the scene. Frightened screams filled the air, along with the shouts of individuals trying to take charge and bring the situation under control. Moments later, the wails of emergency vehicle sirens could be heard in the distance.

"Wade," Tanya groaned as soon as her heart started to beat again. "Get off me. I can't breathe."

He pushed himself to his knees. "Are you okay, Tanya?" he asked, staring down at her anxiously.

"Oh, wonderful," she muttered, sitting up and flopping back against the passenger door of a bright blue Taurus. "Did your truck just go boom, or was that a figment of my overactive imagination?" She started to climb to her feet for a better look.

"Get down," Wade growled, yanking her back down on her knees. "If whoever did that was watching, they know they missed us. Watch out for sniper fire."

She stared at him in white-faced shock as his words sunk in. "Oh my god," she whispered through wooden lips, stiff from the cold chill of fear spreading rapidly across her body. "Someone just tried to kill us, didn't they?"

He nodded grimly. "I guess Turvey was right." He rubbed one hand underneath the collar of his jacket, shaking his head to knock a few stray pieces of car window from his hair. "Thank God for safety glass."

"W-what do we do now?" she gulped. "Do you think someone will try to shoot us if we get up?"

He frowned, considering the situation. "Not if we mingle with the crowd that's no doubt gathering around what's left of my truck. The police should be here any minute, and then we can sneak away in a cruiser. Stay put, while I take a peek."

Wade slowly raised his head over the hood of the blue Taurus. "Oh shit!"

"Let me see." Tanya lifted her head up beside his. "Wow! There's nothing left of it."

He spotted Agent Turvey exiting a vehicle that had just screeched to a stop at the scene. "See Turvey over there?" he asked, pointing with his finger. "Let's try to make it over to him. He'll get us out of here."

They slipped into a small crowd of curious onlookers moving in for a closer look at the action. Careful to stay hidden in the center of the group, they made their way over to where Wade's truck used to be.

Turvey had his back to them as he spoke into his cell phone. "There's no way anyone could have survived it, sir," they heard him say. "It looks like—."

Turvey broke off midsentence as Wade stepped into his line of sight. The FBI agent stared at the two of them in surprise for a few seconds and then an expression of intense relief crossed his face. "I'll have to call you back," he instructed the person at the other end of the line, before shoving the phone into his jacket pocket.

"You weren't in the truck?" he asked, though it was really more statement than question.

"No, a runaway grocery cart hit the truck while we were still far enough away to escape the blast."

Turvey whistled. "Talk about a lucky break."

Davis pushed his way through the crowd toward them. "What the hell happened?" he demanded.

"Somebody missed," Wade informed him dryly. "Do you still think Tanya should go back to her apartment?"

"Uh, of course not," Davis agreed. "You guys had better come with us."

Wade turned to Tanya. "You go with them. It's safer that way."

"What about you?" she demanded.

"I have something I have to do first," he answered, the determined glint in his eyes telling her he was still planning to check out Starbright Enterprises.

Well, if he thought he was going to do it on his own, he had another thing coming. "I'm staying with you," she announced.

Wade stared at her in surprise. "You can't be serious. Someone just tried to kill you!"

"Yeah, well they tried to kill you, too, and I don't see you running to the FBI to save you."

"It's different with me," he began, and then exploded into anger at the now-familiar argumentative expression sliding across her features. "Look, Tanya, you'll be safer with them. I don't know how much longer I can keep you alive on my own."

"You've done just fine so far," she began.

"Listen to Mr. Scott," Agent Turvey interjected. "We know what we're doing."

Tanya glared at him, resenting his implication that Wade did not. Her glance slid past him to his partner, who was eyeing her almost predatorily, no doubt remembering how hard she had bitten him. She shuddered, the thought of driving away with that creep giving her the heebie-jeebies. "I want to stay with you, Wade."

"No!" he shouted in exasperation.

"You can't make me go with them," she shouted back.

"No, you can't, Scott," a masculine voice interjected mildly.

Tanya spun around. "Detective Jansen. Fancy meeting you here."

Jansen nodded a greeting. "But in this instance, I agree with him, Ms. Riverton. You would definitely be safer under police protection."

"No!"

"Or alternatively, you could get out of town for a while," he continued as if she hadn't interrupted.

"They'll just track me down and kill me," she sighed in resignation. "Whatever I know, I wish I didn't." She looked over at Wade, her eyes beseeching him to give in. "Wade, please."

His eyes softened at her desperate plea, and she sensed his wavering resolve. Grabbing his arm, she tugged him aside from the others. "Wade, don't make me go with that horrible Davis," she whispered, her expression earnest. "Let me stay with you. I know you're going after those creeps that tried to kill us, and I want to help. I won't get in your way, and I promise I'll be vewy, vewy good."

He burst out laughing. "All right." He surprised himself by agreeing. In all honesty, he was just as loathe to leave her in Davis's hands as she felt about being thrust into them. Their brief conversation in the mall's security office had given Wade the distinct impression that her safety was not really that high on either FBI agent's priority list, and he strongly believed he would be more committed than they to protecting her in a hostile situation.

"Forget it, Scott," Turvey challenged. "She's coming with us."

"No, she isn't," Wade informed him bluntly, taking exception to the other man's tone.

"Yes, she is," Davis jumped in.

"Am not," Tanya argued back, barely resisting the urge to stick out her tongue at the two agents. Like Wade, she resented their peremptory manner.

Davis took a step toward them, and surprisingly, it was Jansen who came to their rescue. "Back off," he warned. "Unless you arrest her, you can't make the lady go with you."

Davis turned to Jansen with a hostile glare. "Stay out of this, Detective, or you'll regret it."

Jansen raised an eyebrow. "This is going to make an interesting report," he commented lightly. "Truck blows up. FBI agent threatens intended victim, and then threatens local police detective. Meanwhile, bad guys get away. Yep, that's going to make my captain feel real cooperative toward you guys, don't you think?"

"We get the point, Detective," Turvey informed him, giving his partner a warning look. He pulled out a card and handed it to Tanya. "If you change your mind, Ms. Riverton, this is where you can reach me anytime, day or night."

Tanya accepted the card and shoved it in the back pocket of her jeans. "Thank you, Agent Turvey. So long, Agent Davis," she cooed, wiggling her fingers at him.

Davis turned on his heel and disappeared into the crowd, with Turvey following close behind.

"Thank you, Detective," Tanya said to Jansen.

"Just doing my job, ma'am," the man answered. He looked at Wade. "Would you folks be kind enough to come down to the station with me and fill out a complete report on what happened?"

"Sure thing, Detective."

The three of them climbed into Jansen's unmarked patrol car and headed to the police station. Tanya and Wade were separated into two different rooms while each recounted their own version of what happened. By the time they were through, it was well past the dinner hour.

"Would you like me to arrange a lift back to your apartment?" Jansen asked Tanya politely.

"No, I don't want her to go back there," Wade interjected. "It's too dangerous."

Jansen nodded his agreement. "Where will you take her?"

"Wait a minute. Don't I have a say in this?" Tanya demanded.

"No," Wade told her. "You promised to be good and not get in the way."

She obediently clamped her mouth shut and began to count slowly from one to ten, silently fuming over the parental tone he was taking with her. But a deal was, after all, a deal.

Wade turned his attention back to Jansen. "Any suggestions?"

"For tonight, some place public, outside of Bellevue. Maybe a downtown Seattle hotel. But check in under a different name."

"So does this mean you think Wade's a good guy now, Detective Jansen?"

"Some bad guys will go to great lengths to make themselves look good," he informed Tanya. "They might even blow up their own truck."

Wade snorted, making his opinion of that statement clear. "Say Jansen, the detonator on the bomb was obviously some kind of motion detector. What was used for the one that killed my brother-in-law?"

Jansen didn't respond, but the expression on his face gave Wade his answer.

They called a cab from the station, which dropped them off at the Best Western on Taylor Avenue, not far from the Space Needle and Seattle Center. Tanya walked through the front doors on Wade's arm, and then much to her surprise, was lead back outside again.

"What's going on?" she whispered from the shadows where Wade had positioned them.

"I'm not taking any chances," he answered, waiting for the right opportunity to make his move.

It came as a different cab company dropped off a batch of noisy patrons. Before the rear door of the cab swung shut, Wade and Tanya jumped into the backseat. "Take us to the Ramada Inn at Blanchard and Fifth," he ordered the surprised cab driver.

Once they arrived at the hotel, Wade checked the two of them in as Mr. and Mrs. Saunders.

"When can I go back to my apartment?" Tanya asked as they entered their suite.

"You can't. It may be wired to blow as well."

She gasped as a terrifying thought struck her. "What about Charlie?"

"Forget the cat."

"But I can't just leave him there to starve. Aside from you, he's all I've got." Two tears rolled down her cheeks at the thought of her sweet, affectionate Charlie slowly starving to death, and she began to cry in earnest. "I have to save him," she announced, wiping her eyes and heading for the door.

"Tanya! Don't be an idiot." He grabbed her by the arm. "People are trying to kill you."

"That's not Charlie's fault. He's my baby. He needs me," she insisted, yanking her arm free. "I'll never be able to forgive myself if I turn my back on him now."

"Okay. You win. I'll go get him."

She shook her head. "I can't ask you to do that. Charlie is my responsibility."

"And you're mine." He sighed, brushing the tears from her cheeks with gentle fingers. "Listen, Tanya, I know it's been a hell of day for you. For both of us. But please, just sit down a minute and listen to me."

He led her over to the edge of the bed and she sat down with him. He put his arm around her, and she leaned into his warm strength. "Even if the bad guys go to your apartment, Charlie is going to be perfectly safe. They wouldn't hurt him, because then we would know they'd been there. So you see, he'll be perfectly fine on his own for a couple of days."

"But what then?" she asked. "I'm going to have to go get him eventually."

Wade didn't argue her point. He couldn't. "Okay. Here's the deal. You stay put here and don't open the door for anyone until I get back. I'm going to rent a car and go get Charlie."

"Thank you, Wade." She gave him a huge bear hug. "But please be careful. Maybe I should come with you to watch your back."

"No way. You stay put."

She began to worry the moment he shut the door behind him. Guilt plagued her as she considered the possibility of Wade losing his life over a cat. His logic about them not hurting Charlie made more and more sense the longer she considered it. Perhaps she should have listened to Wade and let Charlie be for a few days. And yet, how could she leave her poor baby to fend for himself?

Aside from Wade, Charlie was the one other living being in her life she knew she could count on for love and affection. Not that Wade loved her, of course, but he at least liked her a lot. It was obvious the way he treated her, the way he protected her. Like the way she had to protect Charlie.

The more she tried to rationalize her need to see Charlie safe, the more confused her reasoning became. Charlie was just a cat, she told herself as she paced back and forth in the tiny room. *Yes, but he's your cat*, a voice inside her head argued back. How could she allow a man like Wade to risk his life over a simple cat? *How can you not for Charlie?* the same voice whispered. What made her care about Charlie so much? *What difference does it make?* You can't rationalize love, she finally realized. It just happened.

Was love what she was beginning to feel for Wade? Whatever she felt, it certainly wasn't rational. She barely knew him, and though he hadn't exactly lied to her outright, he had flagrantly misrepresented the truth about who he was until detective Jansen had forced his reluctant confession. She ought to be seriously mistrustful of him, and yet had she not practically begged to remain with him this afternoon rather than be placed under FBI protection? Where, pray tell, was the rationale in that?

She paused her pacing midstep, asking herself why just thinking of him was making her feel all warm and cosy inside. It could be simply that her total dependence on him at the moment was coloring her perspective. He was her protector in a world of fuzzy confusion, the one known variable in a sea of unknowns, and she was desperately in need of something or someone to believe in. Perhaps when this was all over and her memory returned she would be happy to see the last of him.

The thought of saying a permanent goodbye to Wade elicited a tiny whimper of protest, and she dropped down onto the bed, perilously near tears. Her mind stubbornly refused to consider the possibility of him leaving; she just didn't have the emotional strength to deal with it at this particular moment. Grabbing the remote control, she turned on the television and began flipping through the channels.

Time passed with agonizing slowness. Every few minutes she checked her wristwatch, wondering how long it took to rent a car, drive to her apartment and grab Charlie. She began to pace again, debating whether or not to phone detective Jansen and ask him to go find Wade and make sure he was all right.

Nearly two hours went by before she heard a key in the lock. She raced toward the door, almost sick with relief. A horrible moaning sound stopped her dead in her tracks, her hand frozen on the doorknob. Had they captured Wade, tortured him into telling them where she was, and were now coming to get her in order to finish them both off?

She backed slowly away from the door, looking for a place to hide. The closet appeared to be her only option, and she leaped inside, sliding the door shut just as the main door opened and closed again. She heard the dead bolt turn in the lock.

Tanya stood as quietly as she could in the darkness, her heart pounding so loudly she feared it would give her away. She heard another moan and cringed, closing her eyes in sympathy. Poor Wade. What on earth were they doing to him?

"Tanya? Where are you?"

Her eyes snapped open wide. Wade's voice was strong, and filled with urgency as he called for her. He obviously was not the one being tortured. Perhaps he had captured one of the bad guys and been exacting some well-deserved revenge. If that were the case, she sure as heck wanted to help.

"I'm in here, Wade," she called out. He slid the door open, and she popped out of the closet, her eyes glowing with bloodlust. "Where's the snake? I want to punch him one right in the kisser."

Wade stared at her blankly. "What are you talking about?"

"That moaning sound. Didn't you capture someone?"

He burst out laughing. "That's Charlie," he chortled.

"Charlie?" she gasped. "What on earth have you done to him? Where is he?"

"In there." Wade pointed to the kitty outhouse on the floor in front of the door. Another pitiful wail erupted from inside. "I had to borrow your neighbor's welcome mat to block off the opening," he explained. "I was afraid to touch anything inside your apartment other than Charlie and his litter box. I figured no one would wire that, because the cat might accidentally set it off before we got home."

Tanya knelt down, flipped open the latches and lifted the lid. Out popped Charlie, his fur covered with kitty litter. His eyes blinked a couple of times at the sudden brightness, and he howled once more in protest.

"Baby! It's okay. Mommy's here," she cooed, and Charlie swung his head toward the sound of her voice.

"Meow?" he questioned and leaped into her arms, nuzzling his head against the bottom of her chin affectionately.

"That's right. You're safe now," she assured him as she began to pick bits of kitty litter out of his fur. "Thank you, Wade," she smiled at him gratefully.

"Hmph," he grunted. "I don't think Charlie's feeling particularly thankful at the moment. The damn cat tried to bite me."

Charlie hissed in his direction.

"Don't worry, he'll get over it soon enough. Charlie never holds a grudge for long."

"Yeah, well, I hope he likes hamburgers. I stopped at the drive-through on the way back here." Wade pulled a McDonald's bag out from underneath his jacket. "Thought you'd be starving by now. I know I am."

Charlie caught a whiff of the food and leaped down from Tanya's arms. "Meow?" he asked Wade in his most friendliest of cat manners.

"See, you're best friends now," she laughed.

Wade opened the bag and removed a plain hamburger. He undid the outside wrapper and laid it on the carpet, breaking the burger into tiny chunks on top of it while Charlie rubbed up against his legs, purring loudly. He stepped back, and Charlie began at once to devour his unusual but entirely acceptable dinner.

The two of them munched on a couple of Big Macs as Wade filled her in on why he had taken so long to collect Charlie.

"I got the car and drove around a bit to make sure no one was following me before I went back to your place. I didn't want to use the door in case it was wired to blow, so I climbed up onto your balcony the same as I did the other day, going up the far side where it's mostly sheltered by trees. By then, it was pretty dark so I doubt anyone saw me. The outside glass appeared to be untouched, and so I took a chance and pried my way in with the tire iron from the trunk of the rental car. Then I grabbed Charlie and stuffed him in his kitty outhouse. When he wasn't too cooperative, I borrowed Martha's welcome mat from her balcony and used it to block the opening. Then I high-tailed it out of there."

She smiled mistily at him. "Thank you again, Wade, from the bottom of my heart. I'm so sorry I made you risk your life for Charlie. I'll make it up to you one day. I swear."

He leaned forward and wiped a dab of sauce from the corner of her mouth. "Don't worry about it," he assured her, his tone as soft and gentle as his touch.

She stopped eating and started feeling that warm and fuzzy sensation again. He immediately picked up on her sudden change of mood, and they stared deeply into each other's eyes for a long moment, both silently communicating their mutual attraction to each other. The problems of the present faded into oblivion, and for a brief moment, something magical flared between them.

Charlie jumped into her lap and began sniffing at the corner of her Big Mac, breaking the spell.

Wade stood up and grabbed the local newspaper from where he had tossed it onto the bed earlier. "I bought a paper downstairs. Thought I would make a few calls this evening to see if I could find us a furnished place to call home base for a while."

While Tanya cuddled Charlie, Wade began making phone calls, explaining to the various landlords that he was looking for immediate occupancy of a furnished place for several months while he completed a construction contract here in town. After several dead ends, he finally met with success.

"I've got a place," he told Tanya as he hung up the phone. "It's a fully furnished condo on the north side of Queen Anne that allows cats. I'll give the deposit to the landlord first thing tomorrow morning, and then we'll get out of here."

"Okay," she told him agreeably. "Then what?"

"We have to check out Starbright Enterprises. It's our only lead so far." He sighed. "I really wish you'd gone with the FBI today, Tanya. Things are going to really heat up from here on in."

"Don't start that again," she warned.

"For Pete's sake, Tanya. You just don't get it, do you?" he accused her angrily, smashing fist into palm in frustration. "We're not playing games here. At any moment, hit men could burst through the door and mow us both down. Charlie too," he added, pointing at the cat for emphasis.

She cringed at his obvious fury and started to cry softly. "I'm sorry, Wade. Please don't yell at me. I only wanted to be with you," she admitted in a shaky voice, her lips trembling as she stared at him with huge, teary eyes. "Wade, I . . . "

He swore softly. "I'm sorry, Tanya," he apologized, crossing the room to take her in his arms. He kissed the top of her head as he held her close, rocking her gently. "Hush, sweetheart. I'm only angry because I'm worried about your safety. I care about you, you know."

"Do you really?" she whispered, standing on tiptoe to press her lips against the hollow of his neck. "Show me."

He stiffened. "Tanya," he groaned painfully, setting her away from him. "We shouldn't do this. It's business only, remember? You said so yourself."

"I changed my mind," she told him, her eyes glowing darkly brilliant, revealing the depth of her desire for him. "Make love to me, Wade. I know you want to."

"I don't think that would be a good idea, Tanya," he managed to grind out through clenched teeth, wincing as every inch of his heated body screamed out in protest over his words.

"I do," she whispered again, pulling his T-shirt from his waistband and slipping her hands underneath to caress his burning skin.

He groaned again, this time in defeat, and brought his lips down to claim hers in a searing kiss that reverberated every ounce of his pent-up desire for her. She melted into him and met his passion head on with an equal amount of her own.

He pulled her down onto the bed next to him and began to remove her clothes as he continued to cover her mouth and neck with hot, wet, skin-scorching kisses, making her tremble all over from head to toe. There was no trace of the gentleman he'd been their first time together, for his need was too great to allow for slow and gentle loving. Which was fine by her; she was in no mood for tenderness either. He wasted no time, mounting and entering her almost savagely, barely remembering at the last second to watch out for her bruised ribs. She matched him thrust for frenzied thrust as he brought her quickly to a glorious climax, following close behind with his own gratifying release.

He collapsed on top of her, propping himself up on his elbows as they both waited for their breathing to come back until control. Tanya smiled contentedly as she lay quietly with her eyes closed, enjoying the tiny aftershocks of pleasure still tingling throughout her body. He kissed the tip of her nose and rested his forehead lightly against hers, enjoying their closeness and feeling fiercely possessive of her at this very moment.

Never in a million years would he have guessed that making love to Tanya Riverton would be such a mind-boggling experience. Or that holding her sexy little body against his could feel this damned good. If anyone had suggested it to him a week ago, he would have laughed aloud and declared the idea of snuggling up against the sharp-tongued, nasty witch a fate worse than death. And had anyone told him that once she curbed her acid tongue and sheathed her bloodthirsty claws, she could be quite adorable in a uniquely Tanya kind of way, he would have wasted no time in telling them they were plumb loco. He had begun his reluctant association with her determined to keep things strictly business, his heart hardened in bitter remembrance of the harsh injustices she had dealt him for so many years. But somewhere in the space of a few days, his cold indifference had melted into something that was now starting to simmer at a slow, tantalizing boil. Tanya was getting to him, whether he liked it or not.

He felt a gentle thump on the pillow beside them and opened his eyes to find Charlie staring at him with feline disapproval etched across every inch of his furry face. "Don't you dare hurt my mistress," his hostile expression seemed to say.

A sharp stab of guilt pierced through him as he considered again how Tanya was going to feel about their lovemaking once her memory returned. But things had changed between them, hadn't they? She would be willing to bury the past and let bygones be bygones, wouldn't she?

It was obvious Tanya was attracted to him, but just how deep did it go? And what on earth was she going to say or do once her memory returned and she realized who he was? He allowed himself to fantasize for a brief moment that she'd tell him it really didn't matter, despite knowing full well she was going to kill him instead.

If Charlie didn't kill him first. The tubby tabby certainly looked as if he were thinking murderous thoughts at this particular moment. And it wasn't as if those types of thoughts were unjustified. He knew he'd been wrong to make love to her once under false pretenses. But twice? Once was unconscionable. Twice was unforgivable. And that meant a third time was impossible. This must not, could not, happen between them again.

Chapter Eight

"I'm going to tell you this one last time. You're staying in the car. Period. End of discussion."

She started to object to Wade's high-handed manner.

"I mean it, Tanya," he warned. "These people are killers. The only reason you're here is because I don't trust you to wait for me at the condo. I'm going to leave the keys in the ignition. If it looks like anyone has spotted me, I want you to honk the horn once to warn me and then get the hell out of here. Don't wait for me—I'll be much better off on my own if I don't have to worry about you."

"Okay, Wade. I promise." She watched him study her mutinous expression until he was satisfied she would in fact do as she said. "I said I promised," she muttered in a sullen tone as he opened the door.

He swung back with a sigh. "I know you did. It's just that sometimes you're too impulsive for your own good."

"I'm my mother's daughter," she told him with an impish grin.

He frowned at her words. "What?"

"My father always used to tell me I was my mother's daughter," she repeated, giggling at the memory. Her eyes opened wide. "Hey, I remembered something again."

"Yeah, I guess you did. Well, wish me luck."

Wade got out of the car, shaking his head sadly. From what he remembered of Tanya's mother, he hardly considered the comparison a compliment. Mrs. Riverton was at least as impulsive as Tanya, his memory recalled. And there was little doubt in his mind that the woman had provided Tanya with a somewhat distorted version of how Tanya's father had died. She'd certainly downplayed her own part in the unfortunate incident.

He looked back over his shoulder to assure himself Tanya had moved over into the driver's seat and then slipped into the shadows. The thin cloud cover which had moved in late that afternoon was effectively blocking a good portion of the light reflecting off the moon and stars overhead, thus making his trek up the street somewhat easier. The streets were deserted at this late hour, reminding him he wasn't exactly in the best part of town. He wasn't comfortable leaving Tanya alone in the rental car, and wished she'd been willing to wait for him at the condo. But he'd believed her when she threatened to follow him over in a cab. At least he'd parked a couple of blocks away from the Starbright warehouse.

Wade cut around the back of a small building, searching for safe passage to Starbright that would keep him off the street and thus better hidden from view. He took his time, so that several minutes ticked by before he finally reached the warehouse.

There was a light on in one of the front offices, and he slipped up to the window. He saw at a glance that the building was a good many years old, and had been poorly maintained. The wood around the window frame had started to rot away, so that although the window was closed, he could hear the conversation taking place inside.

"All the merchandise has been received and accounted for," a male voice was saying. "It's on schedule to ship out as planned."

"Excellent. I'll alert Johnston. No, don't leave just yet. I'm not finished with you," a second voice responded, its tone hardening on the last sentence.

"What is it, boss?" the first voice asked. Wade thought the man sounded suddenly nervous.

"What exactly happened at Factoria Mall yesterday afternoon?"

"Uh . . . our boys missed the Riverton woman again. A grocery cart slammed into the truck and set off the bomb before they were close enough to get caught in the blast. It just missed them. What are the odds of that happening, hey?" Nervous laughter ensued.

"Who ordered the hit?"

"Dayner arranged for it, sir."

"What the hell for?"

"You mean you didn't ask him to?"

"No."

"Well then, maybe he panicked when he found out the girl was on to him."

"Who told him?"

There was a slight pause. "Fergus did. Dayner overheard us talking about going after her again, and he wanted to know why. So Fergus told Dayner she'd hired Cliff Peterson to investigate him."

"That was stupid. So now Dayner knows about Peterson."

"Yeah."

"And how did he know to call Ace? I assume that was his handiwork this afternoon?"

"Fergus told him Ace did it."

"Damn. Fergus has a big mouth. If Dayner knows about Ace, then they're both liabilities."

"They're both true believers, sir. They'll do whatever you tell them."

"Well then, tell both of them to back off and do only what they're told to do! And tell Fergus to keep his mouth shut. If he wasn't family . . . "

"Yes, sir."

Dayner," the other man spat, as if it were a curse. "The man's a pain in the ass. Using the same MO on the truck as we did with Peterson's office links the two of them together, which is the last thing we need. There's to be no more assassination attempts on either the woman or the brother-in-law. Got that?"

"Yes, sir."

"Good. Pick them up and bring them to me. Alive. I need to know how much Scott has on us and how much he might have told the police."

"Uh . . . there's a small problem, boss."

There was a slight pause before the boss spoke again. "Well, what is it?" he demanded impatiently.

Wade began to feel a tad bit sorry for the other guy. The boss sounded like his underling was going to have a much bigger problem on his hands at any moment.

"We can't find them."

"What?" the man exploded. "Talk to me, Billy," he added in a dangerously soft voice.

"Well, sir, they apparently left the police station late yesterday afternoon, but we lost them downtown. Our boys thought they checked into the Best Western near Seattle Centre, but there's no one registered under either name, and we've been watching the place for two days without seeing them coming or going."

"Idiots! They obviously snuck out and went somewhere else. Did you think to put a watch on the Riverton woman's apartment?"

"Uh . . . not until this afternoon, sir. When we figured out they weren't in the hotel. Her car's in the parking lot, but the place is empty."

"Damn you, Billy. Well, put a watch on Scott's place too, just in case. And tell our guy on the payroll to search the car rental agencies for

Wade Scott's or Tanya Riverton's license. They might be able to check into a hotel under an assumed name, but they can't very well rent a car without a valid driver's license. We'll track them down that way."

"Okay, boss. Uh . . . anything else?"

"Yeah. I want you to personally make sure Dayner backs off and does exactly as he's told. Nothing more. He's already caused enough damage. He shouldn't have hired the Riverton woman in the first place."

"I don't think he was thinking with his head when he hired her, sir." Wade heard a snicker.

"Yeah, well the dumb blonde turned out to be too smart for her own good. It didn't take her long to put two and two together. Dayner's lovely lady will just have to be eliminated. And if it wasn't for his excellent "fund-raising" ability, I'd have eliminated Dayner years ago. The man's an idiot."

"He is a true believer, sir. He'll do whatever we tell him to."

"Yes, and that makes him useful for the moment. But don't forget Billy, *everyone* is expendable." Poor Billy, Wade thought. The boss couldn't have made himself any clearer.

"Yes, sir. I'll get on it right away. You can count on me, sir."

"I know I can, Billy. Now find the blonde and the brother-in-law. Pronto."

The light in the office flipped off suddenly, and Wade crept deeper into the dense shrubbery growing along the front of the building, waiting to see where the men would exit. Stray branches scraped across his hands and face and caught on his jacket as he pushed his way toward the deepest and bushiest part he could find. The once finely sculptured shrubs hadn't been trimmed in a long time and had since grown together to form a thick blanket of underbrush that, though difficult to traverse, made for an excellent hiding spot. Even if the lights from their vehicles were to swing in his direction, no one would spot him here. He waited for the men to clear out, praying all the while that they would turn in the direction opposite to where Tanya was parked.

Five minutes dragged by, and he began to wonder if he should make a dash for it before Tanya got too impatient with waiting and decided to come looking for him. The sound of a truck starting up around back froze him in place. A number of voices carried over to him as several more vehicles fired to life. A few moments later, two large trucks and two cars exited the premises. Wade breathed a sigh of relief as they turned in the direction he'd hoped.

He scrambled out from the bushes and dusted himself off, pulling a few stray twigs from his hair. He was just about to move around to the rear of the building when he heard the rumbling of a car engine.

He dashed out to the road in time to see Tanya turning the corner at the far end of the street. He ran toward her as fast as he could, waving his hands back and forth over his head as he motioned for her to stop where she was. He had no way of knowing if anyone was still left inside the warehouse.

She halted and mercifully turned the lights off. As he approached the car, she opened the driver's door and threw herself at him.

"Thank God you're all right! You were gone so long I was starting to think they had captured you. Then when all those vehicles pulled out I was certain of it."

He gently pried her from his body and was ridiculously pleased to note that she had been crying out of fear for his safety. Her tear-stained face worked wonders to diffuse his anger.

"Hush, sweetheart, I'm okay. But get in the car quick, because I don't know if anyone else is still inside the warehouse."

Wade leaped into the driver's seat as Tanya ran around to the passenger side.

"Let's get out of here," she announced with feeling.

He put his foot on the accelerator and pulled a U-turn, flipping on his lights once they were moving in the opposite direction.

"What happened?"

He proceeded to repeat the entire conversation between the two men as closely as he could remember it, struggling to suppress his rage as he confirmed they were the people responsible for killing his brother-in-law. "So we now know Dave Dayner is being used to embezzle funds from Pacific Realtors and you found out about it," he concluded. "Dayner found out you know what he's doing and put out a hit on us without clearing it with his superiors."

"I wonder how come no one else figured it out before me," Tanya mused.

"I really don't know," Wade answered back. "But your company deals primarily in commercial real estate, and there must be some pretty large sums being transferred. Maybe he's figured out some way to skim it off the top."

"You could be right. And I guess your plan worked," she told him admiringly. "Those losers have no idea where we are."

"For the moment," he cautioned grimly. "But their 'guy on the payroll' is obviously a cop. Once he gets involved, it's going to get a lot tougher to stay ahead of them. We're going to have to ditch this car, and we won't be able to use any credit cards. How much cash do you have on you?"

She opened her purse and pulled out her wallet. "Forty-five dollars and change."

He swore. "I've got about the same. That won't get us very far. At least I paid cash for the condo, so they won't be able to track us there."

"I wonder if Jansen is the cop they're referring to. He keeps popping up, and he did give the FBI a bad time when they tried to make me go with them."

"That's just what I was thinking," Wade replied grimly. "I should have punched him the other day when I had a chance."

"Yeah, and then you would have gone to jail and I'd probably be dead by now."

Her comment gave him pause, and he glanced over at her. The thought of her dying at the hands of those killers made his blood run cold. Then it began to pump hot and fast. There was no way Jansen or anyone else was going to get his hands on her. He would see them dead by his own hand first.

"You're right," he grunted. "So where do you think we should abandon the car?"

"How about the train station," she replied after a moment's thought. "Then maybe they'll think we left town because we're scared of them. The only thing is what do we do for wheels afterward?"

"Tanya, you're brilliant," he exclaimed, glancing over to her in admiration. "Only I have a better idea. We'll go to the airport and exchange this car for my parents'. They parked their car there when they took Janie's kids out of the country."

She laughed. "That's perfect."

He turned right onto South Michigan Street as he worked his way toward the WA-90. "At this time of night, it should only take about twenty minutes to get there. Billy probably won't talk to Jansen until morning, and by the time he checks with the rental agencies, we'll be long gone with Dad's car."

They drove along in silence, each lost in their own private thoughts.

"Maybe you should call Agent Turvey and tell him what you overheard," Tanya suggested after several minutes had passed. "Then he can arrest those guys, and we can get on with our lives."

He shook his head and then realized she probably couldn't see the movement in the darkness. "He won't be able to do anything, Tanya, because I didn't see either of the men to be able to identify them. All we know is that one of them is named Billy. And both William and Bill are very popular names."

"Oh." She was quiet the rest of the way to the airport.

Wade pulled off the highway and onto the ramp leading to the airport. As they drew near the terminal, he passed a small service station near the car rental return depot. The Instant Cash Machine sign in the window captured his attention, giving him an idea. He slammed on the brakes, backed up, and pulled into the station.

"What are you doing?" she asked, confused by his actions. "You can't mean to leave this car in the airport with a full tank of gas. Won't that seem strange to the cops when they find it?"

"I'm not here for gas," he assured her. "Do you have a bank card?"

"Yes, I remember seeing one." She opened her purse and fumbled inside. "Yep. Here it is."

"Great. Oops," he added as a thought suddenly occurred to him. "You wouldn't by any chance remember your pin number?"

She looked at him blankly. "No, I don't."

"You did okay with the alarm system at your office the other day," he encouraged. "C'mon, give it a try."

She closed her eyes, thinking a moment. "Two-two-five-zero."

"Okay, go with that and see what happens. We're both going to draw as much money as we can from the bank machine inside. That way, it will look like we cleaned out our bank accounts so we could buy plane tickets with cash. Hopefully they'll assume we somehow managed to fly out under assumed names."

She glanced at him sharply. "Are you sure you're not a criminal? You sound like you've done this before."

He laughed. "No, but I read the entire *Hardy Boys* series growing up."

They went inside. Wade placed his card in the machine first and withdrew several hundred dollars. Tanya put her card inside the machine.

"Here goes nothing." She punched in the four digits and held her breath, waiting to see what would happen. Miraculously the machine accepted her code.

"Take out every cent you can. We won't be able to do this again," he warned.

She managed to withdraw almost three hundred dollars.

They climbed back into the rental car, and Wade pulled his cell phone from his jacket pocket. "This may be my last chance to leave a message at the office for a while," he told Tanya in response to her questioning look. "I want to instruct my foreman to check on Janie every day for the next little while to make sure she's all right. I'll tell him I have to leave town for a few days."

Wade made the call and placed the phone back in his pocket. He was about to start the car engine when he suddenly reached for his cell once again. After powering it down fully, he turned to Tanya.

"Check your cell," he said to Tanya. "If it's not already off, then turn it off and leave it off. I don't want to give anyone the opportunity to trace us via its roaming signal, or our plan to make everyone think we've left town won't work. As of this moment, we're dropping off the radar."

Tanya opened her purse and verified her cell phone was fully off. "We're good," she confirmed, sneaking a sideways glance at her companion. Though she admired Wade's strategic thinking, she couldn't help wondering where he'd learned to be so sneaky. Jansen's warning about some bad guys going to great lengths to make themselves look good popped into her head, but she firmly dismissed it. It didn't matter how Wade knew what he knew, she reassured herself. All that mattered was that he was using his knowledge to keep her safe. She absolutely refused to believe that Wade could love her so tenderly one moment and then betray her the next.

Wade drove to the long-term parking area.

"What kind of car are we looking for?" Tanya asked as they began their search.

"A Lincoln. Black," he replied. "I can't remember the license number, but I'll know it when I see it."

It took over half an hour of driving around before they finally located it. Wade parked the rental car a few spots down. They climbed out and walked toward the Lincoln.

"I hate to ask, but do you have a key?" Tanya asked.

"Don't need one," he replied, reaching underneath the rear tire on the driver's side. He removed a magnetic key box from underneath the wheel well. "Dad has a bad habit of locking his keys in the car. So I gave him this for Christmas a few years ago. Works like a charm."

He slid open the key box and removed two keys. He placed one in the driver's door and the locks on all four doors popped open. They climbed in, and he turned the second key into the ignition. The car fired to life. "Let's get out of here."

"Wait a minute." She put a hand on his arm. "Won't the parking attendant think we're stealing this car? It's too early in the morning for any flights to be coming in yet, and there's no one else around."

"You're right," he agreed, angry with himself for not thinking of it first. "We'll have to wait here until the first flights come in. The windows are tinted, so no one will see in even if they happen to walk by. We might as well get some sleep."

Tanya was certain she wouldn't sleep a wink during the few remaining hours before dawn, but she stretched out across the backseat Wade had so generously offered anyway. The last thing she remembered before drifting off was what a gentleman her fellow fugitive had turned out to be. When all this was over, assuming they both lived through it, of course, she would have to make sure he didn't mount up on his white horse and disappear out of her life and back into the sunset from whence he came. She very much doubted that, once her memory returned, she would find another knight as equally hunky as Wade, or one with armor that shone even half as brilliantly as his. Wade Scott was the epitome of every fair maiden's dream, hers included.

The sudden sensation of motion jolted her awake, and she sat straight up, a shot of adrenaline making her heart pound wildly with fear. "What's going on?" she gasped.

Wade glanced at her in the rear view mirror. "Good morning. There's enough movement in the terminal now that it should be safe for us to leave."

She took one look at his pinched features and the dark circles under his eyes and clucked sympathetically. "You didn't sleep at all, did you?"

He sighed heavily, rubbing his tired eyes with one hand. "No," he replied, not quite able to stifle a yawn. "I'll crash for a few hours once we get back to the condo."

They approached the exit, and Wade handed over the ticket sitting on the front dash.

"Rough night flight, hey buddy?" the parking attendant offered.

"Yeah," Wade groaned back. "Guys like me need more leg room."

"Go home and get some rest," the man in the booth called after them as they drove away.

They returned to what Tanya was affectionately coming to think of as their secret hideout without incident. Charlie greeted them profusely as Wade opened the door, rubbing himself against Tanya's legs and meowing so loudly she was sure he would wake the neighbors.

"Hush, Charlie," she scolded gently as she picked him up and hugged him affectionately.

Wade set the dead bolt and stumbled toward the bedroom. "I need to sleep for a few hours," he mumbled. "Do me a favor and keep that cat quiet, would you?"

"Okay, Wade. Sweet dreams. C'mon Charlie. Let's get you some breakfast."

Tanya moved around in the kitchen as quietly as possible while she fixed Charlie a plate of cat food, adding an extra heaping tablespoon of his favorite flavor of Nine Lives as consolation for having been on his own for so long. Afterward, she tiptoed into the second bedroom to try to get some shut-eye herself. She wasn't feeling that tired, but the additional rest would do her a world of good. If they had to move out unexpectedly, who knew when she would sleep again?

But after half an hour of restless fidgeting, she got up and returned to the kitchen to make herself a cup of coffee. A short while later, she was ready to climb the walls. The events of the last few days had her nerves wound up so tight she was unable to relax and sit quietly until Wade woke up. There was absolutely nothing on television, and there was only so much attention she was able to lavish on Charlie before he meowed in protest and hid underneath the couch, his ears and chin no doubt tingling painfully after having been rubbed almost raw by Tanya's diligent scratching.

She wandered aimlessly from room to room, looking for something to occupy her attention. Glancing absently in the bathroom mirror, she did a double-take, eyeing the bandage on her head thoughtfully. Surely it would be okay to remove it now.

She carefully peeled back the tape, wincing as it pulled at the tiny hairs on her skin. Her wound appeared to be healing nicely, but the crusty scab and dark bruising around it gave her forehead a garish look. She pulled her long tresses over the top of the wound. A bang would hide it nicely, she decided.

She played with her hair a bit longer, adjusting it this way and that, trying to figure out the best way to camouflage her injury. It was a dead giveaway for anyone searching for the two of them. Come to think of it, so was the color of her hair. She needed a disguise.

A daring idea formed in her mind, and a sense of growing excitement filled her as she realized what she had to do. She rinsed her face and combed her hair with the brush Wade had bought her on his trip to the local drugstore yesterday morning right after they had moved into the condo. After cleaning her teeth with the toothbrush and paste he'd purchased on the same visit, she peeked into the bedroom. Wade, who was sleeping soundly, didn't stir.

Perfect. The way he was snoring, she would be out and back before he even realized she was gone. She shut the bedroom door to keep Charlie from disturbing Wade and then let herself out of the condo.

Once out on the street, she had an attack of nerves and almost turned back. Her surroundings were unfamiliar, and with her amnesia, she had no way of knowing whether she'd been in this area of town before, or whether she had friends who lived nearby. What if someone called her name? She wouldn't know if the person were friend or foe.

Squaring her shoulders with determination, she chose a direction and moved forward. The sooner she completed her disguise, the safer she would be.

After walking several blocks, she chanced upon a hair salon. Mindful of her limited funds, she stepped inside and enquired hesitantly about the going rates.

"Well," said the woman at the counter, looking at her thoughtfully. "If you're on a tight budget, we could have one of our trainees cut your hair. Under the supervision of a qualified stylist, of course," she added hastily at Tanya's sudden look of alarm.

"I suppose . . . oh, why not," she agreed. Under the present circumstances, economy would have to take precedence over vanity.

The trainee was a little nervous as she examined Tanya's hair. "Are you sure you want me to cut this?" she asked, eyeing Tanya in the mirror uncertainly. "It's so beautiful the way it is."

"Yep," she replied cheerfully. "And color it, too. I've always wanted to be a redhead. Today, I'm in the mood to give it a try."

With another uneasy look at her supervisor who smiled back at her encouragingly, the young woman got to work. She offered Tanya samples of the various choices of hair coloring available, and together, they chose a rich auburn shade. After the rinse had been applied, the trainee led Tanya back over to her workstation in order to begin the actual haircut.

Tanya watched in thoughtful, contemplative silence as her once-golden locks dropped to the floor, wishing the cobwebs would fall from her brain just as easily. It wasn't the first time she'd studied her reflection in the mirror and wondered exactly who was staring back at her.

Other than the fact that she was an only child, her father was dead and her mother lived in Bellingham, that she was the office manager for Pacific Realtors and she lived alone save for her sweet Charlie, she knew little else about the young woman in the mirror. Except, of course, that an unknown enemy was trying to kill her, and that Wade Scott, somewhat of a mystery man himself, had promised to keep her alive.

Who was she, really? What were her hopes and dreams? Did she have any goals, and how close was she to achieving them? She closed her eyes for a moment and tried to conjure up a single goal, hope or dream, but it was too difficult to concentrate on possible past wishes when right now, the sum total of all her current hopes, dreams, and goals were focused on the desire to stay alive one more day. And, of course, to make love to Wade Scott again.

But who exactly was Mr. Wade Scott, anyway? He was holding back something from her, that much she knew. Something he didn't want her to know about him, for whatever reason. Aside from the fact they had gone to school together, she knew virtually nothing else about his past. And each time she tried to glean some information out of him, he so skilfully maneuvered the conversation onto another topic that she didn't realize what he'd done until it was too late. It could be they had some sort of past history he was uncomfortable discussing with her. Perhaps they had dated during high school or shortly afterward, and for some reason, it hadn't worked out for them. But why hide something like that from her? Did he think the knowledge would make her uncomfortable?

Would it? She thought for a moment before acknowledging to herself that no, it wouldn't. Just because they'd had their differences in the past didn't mean either one of them needed to carry a grudge into the future. People grew with the passage of time. Changed their attitudes and their outlooks as they matured. And that meant that what was once unworkable between two people could quite easily evolve into the opposite, given the necessary time for both parties to broaden their perspectives and expand their life experiences. Whatever their past differences, if any, she was confident that with a little effort from both sides, they could easily be resolved.

Abandoning her speculation of the past, she considered what she did know of the present-day Wade Scott. At this point, she had firmly discounted the notion that he might be a criminal pretending to befriend and protect her in order to claim whatever knowledge was inside her head for his own nefarious purpose. He was much too thoughtful and considerate, tender and caring to be anyone truly bad. No, he struck her as definitely more white knight than dark villain material.

But then why was he so closed mouthed about himself? Surely a white knight had no need to keep dark secrets. What could he possibly want to hide from her?

"Is something wrong?"

Tanya started at the sound of the trainee's voice, the anxious tones snapping her attention immediately to the young woman staring uncertainly at her in the mirror.

"What?"

"You were frowning, so I thought . . . well, that maybe you didn't like what you see."

"No, I was just . . . thinking about something else." Tanya studied her new hairdo in the mirror, only just realizing that the cut was almost complete. Already, her hair was falling nicely into the sassy new style. "Hey, I like it."

"You do? That's great!" The young woman looked both pleased and visibly relieved to hear it.

"Yes. I do. I think it suits the new me." Tanya smiled at her fashionable new bob. Sassy, stylish, sexy. And why not? With no past history to influence her self-perception, she could be anything she wanted. Her grin widened. Since she had chosen such a sleek and chic disguise, she might as well have fun playing the part.

Stopping at a drugstore two doors down, she purchased a pair of oversized, funky sunglasses. On her way back, she spotted a sale sign in a family clothing store on the other side of the street, and crossed over for a closer look. She managed to pick up a change of clothes at a very reasonable price, splurging on a few extra pairs of underwear as well. She bought an oversized track suit for Wade, feeling a strange, fuzzy sensation in the pit of her stomach as she paid for it at the checkout. Tanya was surprised that the simple act of purchasing clothes for a man could make her feel so childishly giddy.

But then Wade was no ordinary man, she reminded herself. He was, after all, a knight in shining armor. Her knight. He had rescued her from her would-be hospital assassin, protected her from the rotten scum at Starbright Enterprises, comforted her when fear began to get the best of her, and made love to her so wonderfully the memory summoned tears to her eyes. Yes, Sir Wade was one of a kind. There wasn't an ordinary bone in his body.

It was nice to be able to do something in return, like surprising him with something new to wear, she rationalized. She hoped he approved of her choice.

Feeling very much like James Bond, she entered the coffee shop next door and changed into her new clothing in the restroom. The sign "Washrooms for Customers ONLY" posted on the front of the door to the ladies' room made her feel a little guilty, so on her way out, she purchased a couple of jelly donuts to share with Wade later.

Checking her wristwatch as she rode the elevator back up to the condo, she noted with pride that the entire expedition had taken just a little over two hours. Wade was probably still fast asleep. Boy, was he going to be surprised when he woke up!

She opened the door to the condo and peeked inside. All was quiet. Tiptoeing into the room, she shut the door and set the dead bolt. Her ears picked up a sudden noise behind her. She spun around quickly and crashed right into a brick wall.

Wade grabbed her by the shoulders and shook her, none too gently. "Where is Tanya? What have you done with her?" he demanded, his tone as hard and threatening as his manner.

Her mouth dropped in surprise, and then she burst into delighted laughter.

He released her, frowning at the unexpected reaction. "Who the hell are you?" he demanded, eyeing her warily.

She removed her sunglasses, grinning broadly. "I guess it worked. *You* don't even recognize me."

"Tanya? Oh my god. It *is* you. What the hell have you done to yourself?"

"I'm in disguise," she told him proudly. "Here, I bought you some new clothes."

He automatically accepted the package she handed to him, still staring at her in amazement. "I can't believe it's you. You look . . . great. Fabulous even," he added, smiling with reluctant admiration. But then his smile faded. "You know, you really shouldn't have—"

"But I did, so let's just forget it, Wade," she interrupted. "What's done is done, and there's no point in fighting about it."

He sighed, a long suffering sound. "Guess not."

"Have you eaten?"

"No, I just woke up about ten minutes ago. You could have at least left a note. I was sick with worry," he accused.

She felt a twinge of remorse. "I'm sorry. I didn't even think about it. I had planned to be back here before you knew I was gone, only I got delayed. It won't happen again, Wade. I promise."

He stared down at her earnest expression, the now-familiar feeling of resignation replacing his anger. *Until next time*, he told himself, sighing inwardly. For he knew by now, there would indeed be a next time. Tanya was impulsive by nature; she acted first and thought about the consequences later. That was just the way she was.

"All right. I forgive you." One anxious look from those sweet baby blues and he couldn't possibly stay mad at her. She might drive him crazy at times, but at least she made life interesting.

"Good." She grinned, her high spirits returning now that all was again right in her world. "Come on into the kitchen. I brought you a peace offering."

Intrigued, he followed her and laughed when she plunked the donuts onto a plate.

"Mmm, jelly. How did you know that was my favorite?"

"Good instincts. I'll put on the coffee," she told him, ridiculously pleased that he approved of her choice.

The afternoon passed slowly as they waited for daylight to disappear so that Wade could return to the warehouse and hopefully discover what type of merchandise was hidden inside it. Tanya put up only a token fuss at being told in no uncertain terms that she would not be accompanying Wade on his spy mission that evening. Though she would never admit it to Wade, she'd been scared stiff sitting in the car last night all by herself, waiting for him.

"Whatever is hidden inside that warehouse, people have already died over it. And whoever is behind all this will not hesitate to add another casualty to the list. Or two. If I'm not back by morning, I want you to call Agent Turvey and tell him everything you know."

"Yes, Wade. I promise," she assured him solemnly.

He studied her serious expression, deciding that her surprisingly easy capitulation was genuine. "Okay."

"But you better come back," she ordered tearfully, hugging him close to her.

He returned the pressure of her hug, enjoying the feel of her soft, warm body pressing against his. He would have liked to do more than just hold her, but it was essential that his mind be clear for the dangerous task ahead of him. For if he were to get caught snooping around the warehouse tonight, he'd be a dead man for certain.

"Don't worry about me, sweetheart. I'll be back."

The hours dragged by with agonizing slowness from the moment she locked the door behind him. She sat glued to the television, desperate for distraction, but nothing was able to hold her attention for any appreciable length of time. Before long, she was checking her watch every fifteen minutes, saying a little prayer for his safety each time she did so.

Not bothering to waste her time trying to sleep, she waited impatiently on the couch for Wade's return. The display on the DVD player was glowing 2:34 a.m. when she finally heard a key turn in the lock.

She was halfway across the room before a sudden thought that it might not be him halted her in her tracks. She glanced around desperately for a weapon, just in case. The only thing she could see was the empty juice bottle she had left sitting on the coffee table. Doubling back, she grabbed it, figuring that if necessary, she would knock the bottom off of it just like she'd seen in the movies and cut her foe to ribbons.

The door started to swing open, and she held her breath, hoping for the best but fearing the worst. Wade stepped into the room and whipped the door shut, locking it immediately and leaning heavily against it.

"Wade, what is it?" she cried out. "Is something wrong? Are you hurt?"

He turned toward her, and she saw that his face was extremely pale. She shivered with sudden foreboding, and her heart began to pound with wild anxiety. Something was indeed terribly wrong.

"It's a good thing you managed to get yourself such a good disguise today, Tanya," he told her in a strangely hollow voice. "The warehouse is full of automatic weapons. Cartons and cartons of them."

Chapter Nine

"Oh my god!" Tanya gasped. "Did anyone see you?"

"No. There were a couple of guys on guard duty, but they weren't paying much attention to anything other than their card game. They obviously weren't expecting company."

Wade shifted his weight from the door and moved into the living room. He sat down on the couch, settling back in the soft leather with a heavy sigh. She followed suit, snapping off the television with the remote.

"We're in the middle of something really big, Tanya. No wonder the FBI is involved. Those guns are a threat to national security if I ever saw one."

"I wonder who and what they're for."

He shrugged. "I wish I knew."

"So what do we do now?" she asked, and then laughed, despite the seriousness of their situation. "How many times have I asked you that this past week anyway?"

He smiled with grim humor. "Too many. But I was thinking about it on the way home. Our best lead right now is Dayner. If he's really as much of an idiot as Billy's boss seems to think, perhaps we can use him to lead us right to the ringleader."

She shuddered. "Are you sure that's what we should do? We're liable to get ourselves shot full of holes from one of those guns at the warehouse."

"I know. But unless we get more information than what we already have, we're sitting ducks. We have no idea who's after us or what they look like, so it's only a matter of time before they grab us. And the odds are we won't know that we're in danger until it's too late to run."

"You're sure we shouldn't call the FBI? I mean, now that we have hard evidence with the guns . . . " she offered hesitantly.

He shook his head. "We're not key witnesses to anything. So why would they want to protect us? I still think they'd turn us over to the local police for protection, and then we're a target for the crooked cop."

"We'll tell the FBI about Jansen, then."

"We don't know for sure Jansen is the one. It could be anyone on the force, Tanya. How do we know that the cop assigned to protect us won't put a bullet in us both the second we turn our backs on him?"

She stood up and began pacing back and forth in frustrated agitation. Wade's argument made perfect sense, much as she would have preferred otherwise. Although playing James Bond had been fun at first, the novelty was now starting to wear a little thin as the seriousness of their situation became increasingly apparent. With the stakes growing higher and higher, their options had been narrowed down to only two alternatives, and frankly, she didn't like either one of them. They could go on the attack as Wade suggested, or sit back and wait to die. Two options, but only one real choice.

"Okay. I agree." She sat back down beside him. "So what do we do?" she repeated.

"We'll pay Dayner a visit, and see if we can scare him enough to go running to the big boss."

"And we follow Dayner to find out who the boss man is," she supplied, catching on.

"Right." He stood up and held out a hand to her. "But first we both get some shuteye." She took his hand and allowed him to pull her to her feet. "Yeah. Sweet dreams," she joked.

He laughed without humor. "Right. I'm sure we'll both sleep like innocent babes."

She started to head toward the bedroom but then turned back to him, an unspoken invitation reflected in her eyes. She really did not want to sleep alone again tonight. "Wade, I . . . " she began, her tone hesitant.

He seemed to understand, for he opened his arms wide. She leaned into his warm strength and he gave her body a comforting squeeze of reassurance. "Try to get some sleep," he whispered. "Things will look a lot better in the morning. Trust me."

"I know," she whispered back, smiling to herself as his lips touched the top of her head. She did trust him. She had no choice.

* * * * *

She was back in the driver's seat of the car parked in the shadows of the building not far from the Starbright warehouse. The eerie silence was almost deafening as the stillness of the night closed in around her, thick and heavy with an air of foreboding. A sudden sense of panic surged through her, and she cowered down low in the seat, the heart-stopping, lung-crushing fear making it difficult to breathe.

Suddenly, Wade appeared in front of the car, and she almost cried with relief. Everything was going to be all right; her courageous champion had returned to protect her from those who would do her harm. He was her knight in shining armor, and she felt the calm strength of his noble presence reach out and gently wrap itself around her in a gentle caress of reassurance. Her fear vanished at once and was replaced by a warm and fuzzy sense of wellbeing and a certain knowledge that all was again right in her world. Joy filled her soul and tears of pure happiness streamed down her cheeks, for she hadn't felt this way since—

The sound of gunfire caused her hand to freeze on its way to the door handle, and she watched helplessly as Wade's body stiffened and then shook violently as the force of the bullets ripped through him. Blood spurted from his torso as he reached out to her, his eyes vacant and unseeing.

She jumped out of the car and raced over to his side. "No! Don't leave me," she begged. "Don't leave me like he did."

She looked up and saw three men drawing near, cold purpose emanating from their faceless bodies. All three were armed with an automatic weapon in each hand, the noses of the guns pointing toward the ground and their barrels tracing a semicircle through the air as the men swung their arms with casual indifference. She watched in horror as they slowly raised their weapons, pointing them directly at her. At any moment now they were going to fire . . .

Tanya opened her eyes and knew a moment's panic until she realized where she was and that the terrifying vision had been nothing more than a nightmare. The smell of freshly brewed coffee registered, and she sighed with heartfelt relief, her body relaxing. Her courageous and noble knight was still with her.

She lay quietly in bed for a few moments, thinking back to the dream that had caused her to awaken in such a state of panic. She shivered, recalling the intensity of the fear she'd felt before Wade had appeared on the scene. No doubt it was a reflection of just how much she was afraid that the people after her for real might in fact catch up with her and blow her to bits like they did Cliff Peterson's office and Wade's truck.

It was interesting how quickly her fear had vanished upon seeing Wade. It showed her that despite any remaining reservations her conscious mind might have about his motive for staying with her, subconsciously she trusted him completely. Trusted him to take care of her while her memory was gone and protect her from their unknown foe.

What was it she had called out to Wade as he lay dying in the street? *"Don't leave me like he did."* Now what on earth could that have meant? Had someone else once walked out on her in her hour of need? If so, who could it have been? A friend? A lover? A husband, perhaps? She closed her eyes and searched for a possible answer, but her mind remained frustratingly blank on the matter. Wade might be able to tell her, but she was hesitant to question him. How could she explain her reason for asking without giving away her growing feelings for him?

It seemed crazy that she could feel so strongly attracted to someone she barely knew. The physical attraction was understandable—he was incredibly gorgeous, after all. But what about her desire to spend every waking moment in his company? Or the warm, fuzzy feeling a simple smile in her direction elicited?

It would be one thing if Wade were to return her affections, but so far he had shown no sign of doing so. Except for the couple of times they had made love he'd kept his distance, offering nothing more than casual friendship along with bodyguard service. In fact, his manner toward her had been almost brotherly.

Sighing in frustration, she threw back the covers and padded out into the kitchen. Wade had his back to her as he jabbed his fork at strips of bacon sizzling away in an oversized frying pan on the stove. His T-shirt fit snugly against his upper body, accentuating his broad shoulders and narrow hips. She stood quietly a moment admiring the shape of him, appreciating the vee of his muscular back as it tapered at the waist and curved into a tight derriere. His damp hair told her he'd already showered, and the faint scent of his spicy aftershave permeated through the kitchen. Her mouth watered, and it had nothing to do with the bacon.

"Good morning," she announced, and he turned immediately, smiling as he greeted her.

"Good morning, yourself." His eyes narrowed as he saw the way she was looking at him. He stared back at her for several moments as he struggled with desire of his own. The lightly tousled red hair and sleepy eyes peeking out from that thin little nightgown was indeed a delectable sight, and a very tempting one.

But after what he'd seen at the warehouse last night, he now realized more than ever that he had to keep his mind clear and stay focused on keeping them both safe. And that meant no distractions, especially the kind that Tanya could so easily arouse, with arouse being the operative word. Besides, he was already dealing with as much guilt as any one man could handle in a single lifetime. At some point, he was going to have to tell her the truth about who he was, but fear was holding him back. Fear that once she knew his true identify she would order him from her life for good. And call him selfish and weak, but he simply did not want to deal with the consequences of that happening. Especially at this particular moment, when she was looking at him like she wanted to rip his clothes off and make love to him right where he stood.

With an effort, he turned back to the bacon. "Coffee's ready. Help yourself."

She sighed heavily as she opened the cupboard door, fighting the hurt welling up inside her at his blunt rejection. Since the night in the hotel room, he hadn't touched her, hadn't given any indication that he was still even the slightest bit attracted to her. This big brother attitude of his was driving her crazy. She simply did not understand it, especially after the magic they had created during their previous lovemaking.

"Don't you like redheads?" she asked, wincing at the hurt tone which came out in place of the light teasing one she had intended.

He froze in dismay. Uh, oh. Tanya sounded perilously near tears. She'd obviously misunderstood what she perceived to be lack of interest on his part. He set the fork down on the counter and turned around once again.

"I would find you desirable no matter what color your hair was, my lovely lady," he began, choosing his words carefully. "However, there's too much at stake here for me to distract myself with what I know would be a very pleasurable experience. I need to stay focused and alert, to keep us both safe. But after this is over, look out," he warned with a wolfish grin.

His words salved her hurt pride but did little to soothe her raging libido. Were all white knights so damned honorable and so disgustingly disciplined? The look on his face told her he was not about to change his mind. He was going to be Mr. Gentleman Hero right to the very end. What did the man do, polish his suit of armor at the crack of dawn every morning?

"Isn't there even a minute little speck of tarnish anywhere?"

"What?" He stared at her in confusion.

"Oh, never mind," she told him grumpily, leaving the empty mug on the counter as she went to the bathroom to take a shower.

The hot water spraying down over her body did little to warm her frosty mood. Wade's rule of no distractions while he was hunting killers was most frustrating, especially when she could sure use a distraction or two herself. The constant worry was definitely beginning to get to her, and Wade's lack of cooperation in the bedroom made her want to scream out in fury at the top her lungs. Instead of feeling grateful for his caring protection, at the moment she was bitterly resenting it.

She knew she was being unreasonable, but she was aware also that stress was causing both it and her childish behavior in the kitchen earlier. But of course, Mr. Hero knew all about that too and would be magnanimously forgiving, which only made it worse. What she needed was a real knockdown, drag 'em out fight. But with Gentleman Wade, what were the odds of that? A one-sided screaming match wouldn't offer nearly the level of satisfaction she was looking for.

She stood a long time in the shower, fighting the impulse to march out into the kitchen stark naked and dripping wet to give him a piece of her mind. But what did she have to shout about? That he should cast aside his sterling silver vestments and put his noble horse out to pasture? To stop caring about her safety and indulge her every fantasy instead? In all honesty, that wasn't what she really wanted. Well, perhaps only temporarily.

The water began to cool, and she twisted both faucets to the off position. As she dried her hair, she reluctantly decided to accept Wade's compromise. He could have his way for the time being, but once the bad guys had been put away behind bars, big brother had better become dream lover.

She dressed and returned to the kitchen, determined to be on her best behavior for the rest of the day. Wade had kept her breakfast warm in the oven, and as she ate it, they discussed their plan of attack.

"It's Sunday, so I doubt we'll find Dayner at your office. I found a phone book while you were in the shower. There are three D. Dayners in it. I was hoping that perhaps if you called, you might recognize his voice."

"I can give it a try," she shrugged.

She dialled the first number. A woman's voice answered, and she asked to speak to Dave.

"I'm sorry, you have Donald Dayner's number," the woman apologized. "Dave Dayner lives on Applebee Crescent."

"Is he the one who works for Pacific Realtors?" Tanya asked, her tone pleasantly neutral.

"Yes, that's right."

"Well, thank you very much. Sorry to have disturbed you so early on a Sunday."

"No problem at all, my dear. We're already up, getting ready for church. Dave will probably be at church today, too. Would you like me to give him a message for you?" she offered politely.

"Oh, no thanks. I'll see if I can catch up with him myself."

Tanya rung off and looked up to see Wade staring at her expectantly.

"Well?" he demanded.

"Dave Dayner lives on Applebee Crescent, but he's probably getting ready for church right now. I wonder if we can catch him."

"Church?" he repeated thoughtfully. "Do you remember me telling you that Billy defended Dayner by calling him a true believer? I wonder if whatever church he goes to is mixed up in this."

"A church?"

He shrugged cynically. "You never know these days, Tanya. And besides, what a perfect setup. Who would suspect the friendly neighborhood clergy?"

"Wow." She shook her head in sad acknowledgment of his words. "Crazy though it sounds, after this past week, I think I'm ready to believe just about anything."

"Let's head on over to Applebee Crescent. It's only just after nine, so we might be able to catch Dayner before he leaves and follow him. "What's the house number in the book?"

She glanced down at the open telephone directory in front of her. "Sixty-eight."

"Let's go."

They dumped the dishes in the sink and grabbed their jackets. She hesitated in the doorway as she spotted her feline friend curled up contentedly on the couch.

"Oh, I forgot about Charlie."

"Relax, I already fed him."

"Thanks." They didn't come any better than Wade, she decided as they took the elevator down to street level. She studied him surreptitiously under her lashes. In addition to being good-looking and in fantastic shape, he was thoughtful, kind, conscientious, considerate, patient, trustworthy, intelligent . . . The list went on and on. He was also handy in the kitchen and more than capable in the bedroom. A prickle of uneasiness tightened momentarily in her stomach. So where was the catch? No one was that perfect.

Everybody had at least one fatal flaw; that was an inescapable fact of human nature. A thin thread of anxiety unfurled in the back of her mind to whisper that perhaps once her memory returned, she would discover his. What then, she wondered apprehensively. Only time would tell, and so far, patience did not appear to be one of her many virtues.

With the early Sunday morning traffic lighter than usual, the drive over to Applebee Crescent didn't take long. There was a dark blue sedan in the driveway of house number sixty-eight, so they parked a few doors up the road and settled back to wait.

A short while later, a dark-haired man in his midthirties exited the house and got into the sedan. Wade cranked the ignition on the Lincoln, and when Dayner pulled out of the driveway and started down the street, he followed behind at a discreet distance. The light traffic made it easy to keep the sedan in their sights without tailing it too closely. Completely oblivious to the Lincoln in pursuit, Dayner drove straight to the parking lot of the Church of the One True Faith.

Wade whistled in surprise. "Say, that's Reverend White's church. His weekly services are broadcast nationally, and he's got quite the following, so I hear. Not only that, but his church has been responsible for spearheading a number of community improvement projects."

"Well then, no one's going to believe us when we tell them he's dirty, are they?"

"It's possible he isn't, you know. Maybe his church is being used as a cover without his knowledge. Just like the management group that owns Pacific Realtors probably doesn't know anything about the checks written to Starbright Enterprises."

"Oh, okay. Maybe you're right. But how do we find out for sure?"

"I don't know." Wade's eyes narrowed thoughtfully. "I think we need to stick with our original plan and try to spook Dayner into running to whoever's in charge of the whole thing. But we can't do that here. If the church is involved in whatever's going on, we're bound to be recognized, and most definitely outnumbered. We'll have to approach him at your office tomorrow morning."

He pulled away from the curb once Dayner entered the church building. "The plot thickens," he commented as he pointed the vehicle in the direction of their condo.

"What do you think the church would want guns for anyway, Wade?"

"It's hard to say, but they can't arm all their constituents one fine Sunday morning and tell them to go out into the street and take over the nation. It just wouldn't work. Maybe they're in it for the money. You know, like wholesale middlemen."

She nodded. "Yeah. Like you said, it's a perfect setup. Who would suspect the church? And if Reverend White's not involved, he's hardly likely to suspect his trusted aides of any wrongdoing, is he?"

"No. Of course not. Their loyalty is first and foremost to God. Or so they claim," he added contemptuously.

"We have to stop them!"

He looked over at her in surprise. "I thought you wanted the FBI to take care of everything."

"I changed my mind. They're not moving fast enough. The American public needs our help," she announced dramatically.

"Give me a break." He rolled his eyes skyward, and she burst out laughing.

"It's Wade and Tanya to the rescue! Well, mostly Wade," she admitted. She held her hand to her heart. "Ask not what your country can do for you, but what you can do for your country."

"Cut it out, Tanya," he scolded, not quite able to stifle a grin. "Let's be serious here."

She stuck her tongue out at him. "What for?"

"Oh, what the heck. Do you think they'll give us a medal of honor?"

"The purple heart, at least."

He grinned again. "Sorry, but that won't be happening. Purple hearts are only given to military personnel."

"C'mon Wade, don't rain on my fantasy," she complained. "They'll just have to make us honorary military then, won't they?"

"It's your fantasy," he shrugged. "But personally, I'd pick a different award if I were you. I don't think purple will go all that well with your hair."

"Oh my god," she told him with mock seriousness. "You're right. I'll have to dye it another color. Maybe I'll become a brunette this time. Oh, and I'll have to go shopping. I'm sure I have absolutely nothing to wear to a medal presentation ceremony."

He chuckled. "You're a typical woman, Tanya. Any excuse to go shopping. But let me guess. Your outfit would be—"

"Purple," they both announced simultaneously.

"We might as well pick up a few items while we're out," Wade suggested once their laughter had subsided. "We need eggs and milk. And more cat food."

They stopped at a grocery store and picked up the necessary items. Tanya spotted a sales bin full of DVDs, and they purchased a couple of movies to occupy themselves for the afternoon. It was shortly after twelve when they arrived back at the condo.

"I'm going to head back over to the warehouse tonight and see if there's any further activity," Wade announced over lunch.

"Can I come, too?" she asked.

He shook his head in the negative as he took a bite from his sandwich. "No way," he told her once he had finished chewing. "It's better that I go alone. There's less chance of one person being spotted as opposed to two."

"Okay." She sighed heavily, secretly relieved but pretending disappointment. After all, it would not do for Wade to think she was a coward. "I'll wait here again."

They put on a DVD and settled back to enjoy it. The comedy soon had her giggling, and she felt the last of the morning's tension slowly melt away. Charlie joined them, curling up in her lap and kneading his paws on her slacks as he purred happily. It could have been any normal Sunday afternoon as they sat together companionably on the couch, and Tanya found herself hoping that the three of them would be sharing many more afternoons like this in the future. It felt like the most natural thing in the world to nestle against the comforting warmth of Wade's body. Natural, and very, very right.

The movie ended, and Wade suggested they save the second one for her to watch later that evening while he was out. He pulled out a monopoly board that he'd found in one of the cupboards and challenged her to a game. She accepted, warning him he was about to lose his shirt.

But by dinnertime, she was forced to eat crow, having mortgaged herself to the hilt and lost all but three of her hotels.

"I never dreamed you could be so ruthless," she complained as they folded the board in half and put it away in the box.

"Business is business," he shrugged, his twinkling eyes belying his otherwise serious manner. "You lost, so you cook dinner."

Grumbling with good-natured protest, she put a frozen pizza in the oven and tossed together a quick salad. "Do you want wine with your pizza?" she called out to Wade, who was watching the news in the living room.

"No, thanks. I need a clear head for tonight. "But go ahead, if you want some."

She opted for Diet Coke instead and opened a can for each of them. "Dinner is served, you ruthless tycoon."

He joined her in the kitchen where they filled their plates and took them back into the living room to finish watching the local news. It was the usual stuff as the city continued on about its daily affairs, oblivious to the nefarious gun-trafficking ring operating on its very doorstep.

Soon, it was time for Wade to leave, and she clung to him with almost desperate intensity just as he was about to shut the door.

"Be careful," she whispered. "Come back to me and Charlie safe and sound, and in one piece."

He kissed the top of her head as he gave her a brief hug. "Don't worry. I'll be careful."

Then he was gone, and she sat down on the couch to begin her lonely vigil. She popped the second movie into the DVD player, thankful for a couple of hours' distraction.

But before the movie was halfway over, she heard a key in the lock. Surprised, she stood up just as Wade stepped inside the room.

"You're back early," she commented, noting his grim expression. "What is it?"

"The guns are gone. All of them. The warehouse is completely empty."

Chapter Ten

"Well, let's hope this works," Tanya muttered under her breath as Wade opened the front door to Pacific Realtors. They were now pursuing their final remaining lead. If Dave Dayner didn't come through for them, they would be right back where they started. And that was practically nowhere at all.

"Amen to that," she heard Wade whisper back as she passed by him. He grinned as she looked up. "I know. That was in poor taste, under the circumstances."

She smothered a giggle. A burst of sunny optimism surged through her as she realized that even if their bluff failed, all would not be lost. After all, she still had Wade in her corner. And what could be better than that?

"Good morning. Can I help you?"

"Good morning," Tanya replied to the receptionist. She removed her dark glasses. "It's me. Tanya."

"Oh, my goodness! I didn't even recognize you. I love your hair. How are you feeling, by the way?"

"Better," Tanya responded. "I'm just stopping by to make sure everyone is doing okay without me."

"Of course, we are. But it's sure nice to see you, anyway. I know everyone will be happy to find out you're all right. We've all been worried about you." The woman glanced in Wade's direction, her gaze speculative.

Tanya ignored her undisguised curiosity, refusing to bite. "Thanks. That's nice to know. C'mon, Wade. You might as well wait in my office while I make the rounds."

Wade flashed the receptionist a brilliant smile as he sailed past her on his way to Tanya's office, leaving the woman looking slightly dazed from the effects of his masculine charm.

"You didn't have to be quite so friendly with the receptionist," Tanya scolded once they were inside her office. "The poor thing looks like she'll be daydreaming about you for the rest of the day."

"Why, Tanya. One would think you were jealous or something," he teased, an amused grin crossing his face.

"Of course I'm not," she retorted with an indignant toss of her head. "Why on earth should I be?"

"No reason at all," he agreed, the teasing glint not quite gone from his eye.

"Excuse me," a masculine voice interrupted. "Tanya, what are you doing here? Aren't you supposed to be taking time off?"

They turned toward the direction of the voice and immediately recognized the person standing in the doorway as the man they had followed to the Church of the One True Faith yesterday morning.

"Good morning Dave. Nice to see you."

Dave glanced over to Wade and then back to Tanya again. "What's he doing here?" he asked, somewhat nervously, she thought.

"We're here to talk to you, Dayner," Wade answered. Though his manner was mild, Dave didn't miss the steely note in Wade's tone.

"What about?" Dave asked, shutting the office door. The man was definitely nervous now, Tanya observed.

"We know about the guns, and we want to cut a deal."

Dave frowned. "What guns?" he asked.

"The guns at the Starbright warehouse on South Hinds," Wade told him impatiently. "Don't play dumb with us."

"I don't know what you're talking about. I swear it," he added quickly, when Wade placed his hands on his hips and gave Dave a menacing look.

Wade sighed in exasperation. "C'mon Dave. We weren't born yesterday, so don't waste our time. I was there. I saw them. We know you're skimming money from Pacific Realtors to finance their purchase."

"I most certainly am not!"

"We have the canceled checks to prove it."

"That money was for . . . " Dave clamped his mouth shut, eyes widening as he realized what he'd just said.

"For what?" Wade demanded.

Dave remained stubbornly silent.

"We're here to cut a deal," Wade continued.

"What kind of deal?"

"Simple. Money for silence."

Dave studied the two of them for a few moments, as if he were judging the level of their resolve. "How much?" he finally asked.

"Two million dollars."

"Two . . . million . . . dollars?" he repeated faintly, staring at Wade with a slightly stunned expression.

"That's right."

"I . . . I don't think you know who you're dealing with here," Dave began, but Wade cut him off with a snort of impatience.

"Of course, we do. We know exactly who we're dealing with or we wouldn't be talking to you now, would we? You tell the big guy we want two million bucks and his personal guarantee for our safety. And you can also tell him we've made a video of everything we know, including footage of the guns at the Starbright warehouse that will be released to every television station in the country if we should, shall we say, pass on unexpectedly. We've also got photocopies of canceled checks drawn on Pacific Realtors' bank account made out to Starbright Enterprises that link you to all of it. So in other words, buddy, if we go down, we're taking you with us."

"Uh, huh." Though Dave was trying to play it cool, Tanya could see he was starting to sweat. She could almost smell the man's fear. "Well, I'll certainly pass the message on folks, but if you want my advice—"

"We don't," Wade interrupted smoothly. "However, I have a piece of advice for you, Dayner. We know the FBI is sniffing around, and that they've probably got your phone lines tapped. So I wouldn't be making any calls to your friends from here or from your place on Applebee Crescent either. I'd talk to them in person, if I were you. Otherwise, you never know what might show up as evidence in the courtroom if the FBI nails you."

Dave, already pale, turned ghostly white. "The FBI?"

"Yeah, that's right. We've managed to get them off our backs, using Tanya's little amnesia trick. She's a pretty resourceful woman, you know."

Dave turned to Tanya. "You mean you don't really have amnesia?"

"Of course not," she shrugged, looking him straight in the eye, rather enjoying his discomfiture. "And by the way, it wasn't very nice of you to order the hit on us. Wade rather liked his truck, until you had it blown up, that is."

His mouth dropped. "Err . . . sorry about that guys. But you know, business is business." He laughed awkwardly.

"No hard feelings, Dayner," Wade replied. "We understand completely. And yes, business is business. All two million of it. We're playing for keeps here, and I wouldn't forget that, if I were you. We'll drop by in a couple of days to arrange a pick-up point for the cash," he added as he moved toward the door. "C'mon Tanya, let's get out of here."

"Wait a minute. How do I get in touch with you?"

"Forget it. We'll call you."

They exited her office, leaving Dave standing by himself in the middle of it. A crowd of well-wishers gathered around Tanya, and she thanked them all, parrying back and forth with them so well that no one would have guessed she hadn't the foggiest notion who she was talking to. Wade stood by patiently, until all at once everyone turned to him, their eyes burning with curiosity.

"We really have to run, now, Tanya," he interjected swiftly, taking her by the arm and propelling her toward the exit. "You don't want to be late for your doctor's appointment."

"I had no idea you were so shy," she remarked once they had left the building. "What's the matter, you don't like being ogled?"

He gave her a speaking glance, but refused to bite. "I figured it was time to get out of there just in case Dave ignored our warning about the FBI and got on the phone to his buddies. Since we don't know what any of them look like yet, it wouldn't be a good idea to stick around long enough for them to get here."

"Do you think it was a good idea telling Dave about the FBI? I mean, I doubt Agents Turvey and Davis would be happy that we told the bad guys the good guys were onto them."

He shook his head. "I doubt that it really matters all that much, Tanya. Since these people have a guy on the 'inside,' I'm sure they already know the FBI is investigating them."

"Well, Dave Dayner sure seemed surprised. I guess he hasn't been told everything."

"That's not surprising, considering the way Billy's boss spoke about him."

They crossed the street to where the Lincoln was parked.

"Now we wait," Wade announced as they settled themselves in the front seat. "And my guess is, we won't have to do it for long. Did you see how scared Dayner was in there?"

"He was absolutely petrified," she agreed, laughing. "Serves him right, for blowing up your truck."

"Yeah," he grunted. "I did rather like the old girl."

Their wait was indeed a short one. Not more than fifteen minutes elapsed before Dave Dayner left the building and ran toward his car.

"Here we go," Wade announced as he fired up the Lincoln and pulled out after the blue sedan.

Dave drove straight to the I-405, headed north and then merged onto the eastbound WA-520. Wade remained on his tail, careful to keep one or two car lengths back to avoid alerting their quarry that he was being followed. A few minutes later, Dave exited the highway at Union Hill Road and worked his way over to 255th Avenue NE.

"Wow! Isn't this a nice part of town," Tanya observed as they passed several sprawling mansions set on immaculately manicured grounds.

The tail lights of Dave's sedan glowed red, and Wade immediately slowed down. Dave turned into one of the driveways. Wade continued past, he and Tanya noting several vehicles in the circular drive.

"Do you think that's Reverend White's place?" Tanya asked.

"I don't know. It could be."

Wade pulled onto the shoulder several hundred feet up the road, taking advantage of a small grove of trees for cover. "Let's wait here until Dayner comes out and then follow him to see where he goes next. I'm going to turn us around so we have a better view of the entrance gate." He put the vehicle back in gear and continued a short way up the street before turning around and parking under the heavy boughs of an ancient oak tree. He figured they were far enough away to avoid suspicion, but close enough to have a clear view of the front gate.

Tanya leaned forward in her seat, peering at the gate intently. "I wonder how long he'll be. What do you think whoever he's talking to is going to say to our offer?"

"I doubt it will be yes," he told her. "And I expect he's going to be mad as hell at Dave for showing up at his place out of the blue. If that is Reverend White's place, he's not going to want to be seen entertaining Dave at his personal residence. I've heard rumors that the Good Reverend is considering running for local office. If that's the case, he'll want to be as far removed from the likes of Dave Dayner as possible."

"Reverend White in political office? Now that's a scary thought."

"Well, it's not going to happen. Not if we can help it. Have you drafted your medal acceptance speech yet?" he asked.

She grinned. "Not completely. But I think I'll ask them to play some James Bond music right after the Star Spangled Banner."

A knock on the window made them both jump right out of their seats. Agent Turvey stood outside, scowling ferociously at the two of them.

Wade looked over to Tanya. "Oops. Some secret agents we turned out to be," he said a little sheepishly as he reached for the electric switch to lower the driver's window.

Turvey leaned inside the vehicle to glower at the two of them. "What the hell are you two doing here?"

"We're taking a drive in the country. You know, to check out how the other half lives."

"This is a lovely neighborhood, don't you think, Agent Turvey?" Tanya added sweetly.

"I'm tired of you two messing around in an official investigation," Turvey growled. "I think I'm going to run you in."

Just then another vehicle screeched to a halt beside them. "Well, well. Look who's here," a voice drawled through the open passenger window. "Hey, guys, what's happening?"

Turvey muttered a curse and stood up straight to face the newcomer. "Hello, Jansen."

Jansen climbed out of his car and sauntered over to poke his head into their vehicle. "And just what are you folks up to today?"

"We're taking a drive, Detective Jansen," Tanya informed him.

"Well, what do you know? So am I. Lovely day for a drive, isn't it? By the way, Ms. Riverton, your new 'do looks great. I like it."

"For Chrissakes, Jansen. Butt out, will you?"

"Butt out of what, Turvey?" he asked innocently. "Say, where's your sidekick?" Jansen looked around. "Hey, Davis!" he shouted at the top of his lungs.

"Shut up," Turvey hissed at him. Then he sighed in resignation. "All right. Let's just everybody get into their cars and drive away quietly before they alert the entire neighborhood to the *covert* FBI investigation going on here."

"I've got no problem with that. Do you, Scott?" Jansen asked.

"None at all, Jansen," he replied.

"By the way, cute trick at the airport," Jansen called back to them as he climbed into his car. He started the engine, but sat there patiently until Wade did the same and pulled away from the curb. Jansen followed behind them.

"Rather odd to see a Bellevue detective taking a country drive in Redmond, don't you think? Seems a little suspicious to me," Wade observed.

"Jansen's got to be the one," Tanya concurred. "It was obvious he was trying to alert everyone to what was going on." A sudden thought struck her. "Oh, oh. Now he knows whose car we're driving."

"I'm sure he's already run the plates," Wade agreed.

"We'll have to ditch it. But how are we going to get our hands on another vehicle?"

He thought for a moment. "There's always my sister's. If we hide this one in her garage, it may take a while before anyone thinks to check her place. It's not the ideal solution, but I'm afraid it's the best option I can think of."

"Okay. I take it you have a key?"

"Yeah. My parents gave me Janie's keys before they left the country. I'm supposed to be keeping an eye on everything while she's in jail."

"Good." She looked back over her shoulder. "Now how do we get rid of Jansen?"

"Hmm. I'm not sure." He glanced in the rear view mirror. "Wait a minute. I think he's turning around. Maybe he thinks Turvey's the greater threat at the moment."

She turned around again. "You're right. Talk about a lucky break."

Wade drove to his sister's place in the Renton area and backed her Buick out onto the road while Tanya drove the Lincoln into the garage. After closing the garage door, he suggested they go inside the house for a moment. "I bet the mail is starting to pile up inside the front door. I want to at least pick up any bills that need to be paid."

He started up the walkway, with Tanya following close behind. He reached for the handle of the screen door, and then froze midstep so suddenly that she crashed right into the back of him.

"Hey," she complained, rubbing the tip of her nose gingerly.

"Damn."

"What is it?" She craned her neck to see past Wade's bulk. "Oh, oh. Looks like someone else has been here."

The front door was indeed slightly ajar, and a closer inspection showed that the lock had been forced open, perhaps with a crowbar or some other similar instrument. Wade slipped off his jacket and wrapped one sleeve around the screen door handle before opening it. He then shoved against the inside door with one shoulder.

The door swung open, and they both groaned with dismay. The place looked much like Tanya's apartment had.

"Well, let's get this over with."

Wade held open the screen door, and Tanya stepped gingerly inside. She wandered into the living room and glanced about curiously, wondering how it would have looked before the cyclone had blown through. A family photograph lying on the carpet near her feet caught her eye. Four happy faces stared out from it; two adults and two little boys, neither one more than two or three years old. A lump formed at the back of her throat. The poor children. They would never see their father again. She reached down for a closer look.

"Hey! Don't touch that," Wade shouted.

She started violently as his words echoed harshly through the silent room and straightened immediately, spinning around to face him. "What?" she demanded, taking offense at both his belligerent tone and disapproving stare.

He glared back at her, suddenly losing patience with her continued lack of forethought. Would she ever learn to curb her impulsive streak? He rather doubted it, somehow. And sooner or later her carelessness was going to cost them both dearly. "For Pete's sake, Tanya. Don't go putting your fingerprints on anything in here. Do you want to get blamed for all of this?"

She raised an eyebrow in askance at the fierce note in his voice. Oh, how she hated it when he was right, which seemed to be most of the time. "No, of course not. But you don't need to be quite so nasty about it, Wade."

"Well, honestly, Tanya. Sometimes you don't even think."

Her eyes flashed fire, and she drew herself up to her full height, placing both hands on her hips as she stared daggers at him. "I do so think! I think just as much as the next person. And right now, I'm thinking you're nothing but a bossy, obnoxious jerk!"

Uh, oh. Now he'd done it. He knew that stance. The Tanya he was regretfully all too familiar with was starting to rear her ugly head. If he didn't take steps to immediately diffuse the situation there was no telling how high she might blow.

"You're right. You're absolutely right." He put both hands out in front of him, palms facing her in supplication as he fought to keep his own anger in check. Though he was sorely tempted to confront rather than placate her temper, he knew he would have to say the words. Even if he choked on them. "I'm sorry. I was out of line just now."

She continued to glare at him a moment longer as the fire in her eyes slowly died. "Yes, you were," she told him in a coolly superior tone. "But apology accepted."

He grit his teeth. Lord, but she could be infuriating when she set her mind to it. "Thank you."

She shrugged indifferently. "You're welcome." She turned away to hide the amused grin tugging at the corners of her mouth. She knew she had sounded the perfect bitch and could tell from the set look on his face that his "thank you" had really hurt. One honestly had to admire his self-control. Served him right, though. So what if she'd acted without thinking? He could just as easily have wiped the frame clean of her prints as shouted at her.

But her momentary triumph felt strangely hollow, for the knowledge he was still angry with her far outweighed her satisfaction of getting the last word in on him. Sighing heavily, she turned around again. "I'm sorry, too, Wade. You were right. I should have thought about the fingerprint thing. It won't happen again. I promise."

He almost laughed aloud at her earnest expression, but formed his lips into a gentle smile of forgiveness instead. "Apology accepted."

"Friends again?" she asked hopefully, holding out a tentative hand.

He laughed softly as he squeezed her hand warmly in his, finding it impossible to remain angry with her. "Friends," he agreed. She really could be quite disarmingly sweet when she wanted.

"I doubt we're going to find anything useful here."

"Probably not," he agreed. "Just give me a minute to walk through the place before we leave. I'd like to make sure everything is at least closed up properly."

He checked quickly through the rooms on the main floor before heading upstairs. A few minutes later, he returned to the living room. "Everything's okay up there. I'm just going to take a look in the basement."

Bored, she wandered into the kitchen to see if it had fared any better than the living room. Standing just inside the doorway, she slowly surveyed the mess and decided it was in even worse shape. Poor Janie was going to come home to quite a disaster.

Something small, dark, and furry raced over the top of her shoe and disappeared underneath a pile of corn flakes. She screamed aloud at the unexpected intruder.

Wade's feet clumped loudly behind her as he pounded up the basement steps two at a time and charged onto the scene. His fists were cocked and ready for action as his eyes darted this way and that, searching for a sign of trouble. They found nothing at all, and his body relaxed slightly. "What happened?" he demanded.

"It was a m-m-mouse," she whimpered, feeling a little silly but still shaky nonetheless. "It ran across my foot and s-scared me. I'm sorry to be so silly." She tried to laugh it off, but to her utter mortification, she burst into tears instead.

"I'm sorry, Wade," she gulped as he stood there looking at her in startled disbelief, his somewhat bemused expression telling her he was having trouble comprehending why such a gusty blond, or make that a redhead, would be frightened by the sight of a harmless little mouse. And under normal circumstances, the mouse wouldn't have fazed her in the least. But though her memory loss made it difficult to determine exactly what normal was, she highly doubted that falling from her apartment balcony, being attacked while lying unconscious in a hospital bed, finding her apartment totally turned upside down, being accosted by FBI agents, narrowly escaping being blown up in Wade's truck, and learning that the person behind it all was a highly respected member of the community, all in the space of a few days, qualified as a run-of-the-mill, average week as far as she was concerned.

It seemed as if the whole world was out to get her, and all of a sudden, one more nasty surprise was too much for her to handle, even if it was just barely the size of her big toe. Uncaring of how childish she must appear to him, she threw herself into Wade's arms and pressed her tear-stained face against his chest. He wrapped his arms around her, enclosing her in the protective circle of his gentle embrace.

"Hush, Tanya. It's all right." He held her quietly for a few minutes as she slowly regained her composure.

Finally, she lifted her head from his chest with a heavy sigh. "Thanks, Wade. I needed that."

"Anytime, sweetheart," he told her gently.

She smiled at the endearment, and on impulse, reached up to touch her lips to his cheek. "You're a very special man."

An answering heat flared to life in his eyes as they locked with hers. Though neither said a word, an unspoken communication sizzled between them for several seconds and continued to smolder until Wade gently but firmly set her away from him. She followed him back out toward the front door, feeling as if she were floating on air. The look in his eyes had said it all. Wade did care for her, even if he was stubbornly refusing to act on it.

They paused a moment while Wade gathered up the mail which had been collecting underneath the slot beside the front door.

"You know, I wonder why they just didn't burn the place down and save themselves the trouble of going through all this stuff."

"They may have wanted to know what evidence Cliff had collected before they destroyed it. And a fire might have tipped the police off that there was something more than drugs involved. This way, it simply looks like vandals have been here. I think some of Janie's jewellery is probably missing. And look, the television is gone."

Tanya eyed the empty stand. "I guess you're right."

Wade handed her the mail and again used the sleeve of his jacket to pull the door shut behind them. "I'll have to get someone from the office to come over here and replace that lock."

"How are you going to get these bills paid?" she asked once they were on the road again.

"I'll re-address them to Able Construction and drop them back in the mail. The girls there will know what to do when they get them."

Tanya fell silent as she thought to herself how lucky Janie was to have a brother like Wade to watch out for her. Especially now that her husband was gone and she would have to raise two young children on her own. She recalled the photo she'd seen at his sister's place. The two little boys had looked adorable. Wade's nephews. Would Wade's children be just as sweet? He would make a wonderful parent, just the kind of father she would want for her own children. What would it be like to have a family with Wade, she wondered, unconsciously tapping the stack of envelopes against her leg as she stared unseeing out the window, deep in thought.

"Do you mind stopping that?" Wade asked. "It's kind of annoying."

"Oh. Sorry," she apologized, glancing down at the envelopes in her hand. The top one was from the phone company. A sudden idea made her ask, "Do you mind if I open this phone bill? You never know . . ."

He glanced at her briefly, nodding his agreement. "Open it."

She ripped open the top and removed the summary of charges within. "Do any of these numbers sound familiar?" she asked, and started reading off the phone numbers of all the long distance calls made during the billing period.

The first few were for various family members, but part way through the list, she came across a number he didn't recognize.

"This is interesting. The call lasted only a few seconds, just long enough to register as a completed connection."

He frowned. "What was that number again?"

She repeated it, and he shook his head. "I don't recognize the exchange."

"Here's another one. This call was only five seconds. Oh, and here's one more. All these calls were made within a few minutes of each other."

Wade didn't recognize the additional numbers, either. They stopped at the Renton public library on Twelfth Street to research the phone numbers on one of the library computers. They were unable to find listings for the numbers, but did manage to determine the three numbers were from exchanges in Arlington, Texas; Little Rock, Arkansas; and Richmond, Virginia.

"Strange . . . I wonder what these numbers have in common," Wade mused.

"Call them and find out," Tanya suggested.

"Not with my phone."

"Then use the one over there. The librarian isn't at her desk, and if I see her coming, I'll distract her."

Wade slowly nodded his head in agreement. "Well, it's not something I would normally do, but under the circumstances, it's probably our safest bet."

Wade dialled the numbers as Tanya kept an eye out for the librarian, who happened to be speaking with another patron at the far end of the room. A few minutes later, he motioned for Tanya to join him, and she followed him back to their computer.

"I called the three numbers, and they all answered 'CFBA.' Any idea what that could be?"

"No," she told him. "We'll have to Google it."

Wade punched the acronym into the Google search screen, and they reviewed the results page.

"Canadian Farm Builders Association... Canine and Feline Behaviour Association... Connecticut Farm Bureau Association... Central Florida Bass Anglers... None of these make sense," Tanya grumbled.

They searched a while longer but came up empty-handed. Just before they shut down the computer, Wade pulled up the yellow pages web site and entered Gerald White into the search engine. A number of entries filled the screen. Wade scrolled down through the list of names.

"Bingo!" he announced as he spied an address on 255th Ave NE. "I think that confirms Reverend White is involved in whatever is going on."

"We didn't learn much, did we?" Tanya commented as they returned to their vehicle, disappointment reflecting clearly in her voice. "So now what?"

"I think we need to pay Dave Dayner another visit."

Chapter Eleven

"Good morning, Dave. Nice to see you again," Tanya commented in a dry tone as Wade shut the door to Dave's office with a decisive click.

"Uh . . . hello, Tanya. Hello, Wade," Dave responded, eyeing them both a little warily.

"So what's the answer to our proposal?" Wade demanded, wasting no time on pleasantries before coming straight to the point.

Dave cleared his throat, a little nervously, Tanya thought. "I've been authorized to offer you half a million in exchange for your continued silence." He held up his hand as Tanya began to sputter indignantly. "I know it's only a quarter of what you asked for," he added hastily, "but I highly recommend you accept the offer. These guys aren't in the habit of negotiating with anyone, I can assure you of that. So I think you should take what you can get, and then leave town, if you know what I mean."

Wade snorted in disgust, the expression on his face telling Dave exactly what he thought of the other man's advice. "We'll accept that as a down payment, I suppose."

Dave shook his head in exasperation. "You really don't get it, do you? The people you're attempting to blackmail could very easily have you killed!"

Wade shrugged indifferently. "And we have enough dirt on them to put them away for good."

"Yeah, right," Dave drawled, his lip curling in disdain. "The guns are gone now, smart guy. All you have is an empty warehouse. Big deal."

"Yes, we know the warehouse is empty, Dave. But we also know all about CFBA."

The sneer disappeared from Dave's face. "How did you find out—?"

A sharp rap on the door cut Dave off midsentence. All three heads spun around as it opened inward. One of the office staff peeked in apologetically.

"I'm really sorry to interrupt," she told them, "but you have an urgent phone call, Dave."

"Who is it?"

"He wouldn't say, but he insisted on speaking to you immediately."

Dave stiffened uneasily, and Tanya and Wade looked at each other in concern. Could he be expecting a call from one of the bad guys, Tanya wondered. What would happen if Dave were to tell him that they were standing in his office right now? Would they have enough time to get away? She could tell by the slight frown on Wade's face that he was thinking along the same lines as she.

Wade tipped his head slightly toward the door. "Don't worry," Tanya told the woman. "We were just leaving. I'll call you, Dave," she tossed back over her shoulder as she moved toward the door.

"Damn. That was bad timing," Wade commented as they left the building.

"No kidding. But maybe we shouldn't have left."

"I didn't think it would be safe for us to stick around, just in case. The person calling for Dave could have been checking to see if we'd contacted him yet. For all we know, they could be sitting across the street waiting for us to turn up. Let's get out of here quickly."

"It's too bad we didn't get a chance to get anything out of Dave."

"Not true. At least we confirmed that CFBA, whatever that is, is somehow linked to what's going on. Did you see the look on his face when I said we knew all about it?"

"Yes, I did. He seemed quite taken aback."

"Too bad we didn't get a chance to get him talking about it."

"Yeah. Well, it shouldn't be that difficult for the FBI to figure out. Is it time to talk to them yet?"

Wade pressed the unlock button on the key fob, and he and Tanya climbed into the Buick. He remained silent, still considering her suggestion as he turned the key in the ignition. "Not quite yet," he responded after a moment, frowning thoughtfully. "We don't know where the guns went, and so we don't know whether the FBI will be able to link them to the people who are after you. We need to find a way to tie these people directly to the guns."

"Can't the FBI do that?"

Wade turned to Tanya, his expression solemn. "I don't know," he told her quietly. "And I don't want to chance it. We don't know exactly who's involved here, other than Dave Dayner and Reverend White of course. So how are we going to know if they miss arresting anyone? We would have no way of knowing whether your life was still in danger or not."

His tone darkened. "Besides, they're not moving fast enough for me. Every day that goes by is one more day my sister sits in her jail cell and one more day her kids have to hide from these creeps. And it's one more day that my brother-in-law's killer remains free on the street," he added grimly, his fingers turning white as they tightened their grip on the steering wheel.

"In other words, you're on a quest for family vengeance," she interjected with a grin, hoping a little humor would help lighten the sudden heaviness which had overtaken his usual good spirits. "Okay, count me in. Let's go kick some reverend butt."

His lips curved upward slightly, but the smile didn't quite reach his eyes, which remained dark and solemn as they connected with hers. "Yeah. Something like that," he muttered, half under his breath.

She reached out instinctively to give his forearm a gentle, reassuring squeeze. "Don't worry about your sister," she told him softly. "Everything is going to work out. You'll see."

He smiled at her again, and this time a corresponding light flickered briefly in his eyes. "I know. It's just that . . . I feel so damned helpless!" he exploded, shoving the gears into reverse and jamming his foot on the gas pedal. The tires squealed as the engine roared to life, and he just as quickly slammed on the brakes.

"Don't be ridiculous!" she told him, grasping the dashboard to steady herself. "Think about it. We're the ones holding all the cards. And it's all because of you. I haven't really done anything. Nor have the FBI, for that matter. So don't you be going on about feeling helpless. You're going to be the one to single-handedly put them all away. I just know it."

He grunted, keeping his thoughts to himself as he maneuvered the Buick out of the parking lot and into the street. A moment later, he glanced down at the dashboard. "We need gas."

"Do we have any money left?"

"No, but it doesn't matter. They know we're still in town, so we might as well use our credit cards."

Wade drove into a gas station a few blocks up the street and filled the tank. As he stood next to the vehicle, gas pump in hand, a momentary lull in the traffic volume revealed what he thought to be the faint sound of an idling engine. Theirs was the only vehicle in the gas station, so he casually inspected the surrounding area. There were a number of vehicles parked in the pay parking lot next to the gas station.

After paying for the fuel, he pulled away from the pumps and back out into the street. From the corner of his eye, he spotted movement in the parking lot. He watched as a dark green SUV exited the lot and turned in their direction.

"Damn."

"What's wrong?" Tanya asked.

"There might be someone following us."

"Do you think they were waiting for us at the office?"

"Probably. They knew we'd be back sooner or later."

"Where are we going?"

"Nowhere in particular, until I know for sure whether or not we're being tailed." He turned right and glanced in the rear view mirror. Sure enough, the SUV turned right as well.

"Are they following?" She swiveled her head to look back over her shoulder.

"Don't look back," he hissed, placing one hand on her shoulder to prevent her from turning completely around in her seat. "You'll tip them off. They're two cars back of us."

"Sorry," she muttered, glancing instead to the side mirror outside the passenger window. It was set at the wrong angle for her to see anything, so she hunched down in her seat and tilted her head to one side.

"What are you doing?"

"I'm trying to see through the side mirror. Hey, the car behind us just changed lanes, and I have a clear view. This magnified mirror is great. I can see the guy in the passenger seat talking to someone on a cell phone."

Wade's brow furrowed in concern. "They might be calling for backup. We better find a way to lose them quick."

He stopped for a red light, and Tanya spied a motorcycle officer stopped on the other side of the intersection, helmet in hand, having what appeared to be a rather heated discussion with a pedestrian. "Hey, I've got an idea. See that cop over there? Pull up beside him when the light changes."

"What for?"

"Trust me. I'm the one who's good at talking, remember?" The light turned green. "Don't argue. Just do it," she insisted when he hesitated in the intersection.

A horn sounded insistently from the vehicle behind the green SUV. She stared at him in exasperation. "Come on. Move it. Or *you'll* be the one giving us away."

"All right," he agreed, sighing as he shrugged his shoulders in resignation. "But the police may not be our safest bet at the moment, you know. I just hope you know what you're doing."

"No problem." She grinned. "Just watch me."

She rolled down the passenger window as he pulled up beside the motorcycle. "Excuse me, Officer," she called out sweetly. The man broke off his conversation and turned to her. She pointed to their tail, which was now passing by them. "You see that green SUV? I think the driver is drunk. He's been weaving in and out of traffic and almost caused an accident a block or so back. You should probably check him out before he seriously hurts someone."

As the officer eyed the vehicle in question it took off like a shot, its tires squealing in protest as they laid down two black streaks of rubber on the pavement. The cop leaped onto his motorcycle and took off after it, his disagreement with the pedestrian forgotten for the moment.

"Hey, thanks, man," the young man called to her from the sidewalk.

She waved in acknowledgement as Wade pulled away from the curb.

"Told you it would work," she advised him in a coolly superior tone.

He chuckled in admiration. "That was quick thinking."

She grinned back. "I do have a few good tricks up my sleeve, in case you hadn't noticed. So now that we've lost our tail, what's next?"

"Let's pick up some groceries and then head home to hole up for a while. I don't want to chance being spotted again. It's starting to get a little too dangerous out here."

She shook her head as a small groan of frustrated resignation escaped from the back of her throat. "C'mon, Wade. Who are you trying to kid? We can't keep hiding forever. It's only a matter of time before they catch us, isn't it?"

He glanced sideways at her, his expression grim as his eyes silently acknowledged the truth of her words.

"Maybe we should call the FBI and tell them everything we know. They might be able to combine their own evidence with what we tell them and come up with enough to take everyone down."

"I somehow doubt it. The FBI obviously knows or at least suspects the reverend's involvement, otherwise Turvey wouldn't have been out at his place the other day. Since there's been no arrest, the guy must be covering his tracks pretty good. My guess is he's far removed from those guns and CFBA, whatever that is."

"Oohhh!" She struck a fist into the palm of her other hand, unconsciously imitating one of Wade's habitual gestures. "I could just scream right now. This is really starting to get on my nerves, Wade. I'd like to chase the reverend around for a change and see how he likes it."

He nodded slowly, thoughtfully. "You know, I agree with you. I think it's time we went on the offensive."

"You mean start following Reverend White around?"

"No. Not quite."

"Well, then, do we go to the press and tell them what we know?"

"No. Not that either. The reverend is a very powerful man, and I don't think anyone in newspaper, radio, or television would publish anything without hard evidence. So," he added, tossing a wicked grin in her direction, "let's go get some."

* * * * *

"You're sure you know how to work that thing?" Wade whispered. "We're going to get only one shot at this."

"Yes, I'm sure," she hissed back just as quietly. "But I still think I should do the talking."

"Forget it. It's too dangerous."

"But you'll be there if he attacks me."

"Yes, but then I'd give the plan away. He can't know we're videoing this."

"All right," she grumbled. "How are we going to get inside?"

"Wait here. I'll find a way in and then signal for you."

He disappeared into the shadows, and she waited impatiently as he worked his way over to the house. She saw him dash across the lawn and slip behind a flowering bush underneath one of the side windows, and then watched as he withdrew something from his pocket. He played with the window for several moments and then lifted it open. She smiled softly to herself in the darkness. Being in the construction business obviously had its advantages when it came to break and enter.

He signaled for her to follow, and her heart began to pound quickly as a shot of adrenaline surged through her veins. This James Bond routine was heady, exciting stuff. The thrill of the hunt was upon her, and her hands began to tremble slightly with reaction. Though her body was aquiver with tension, her mind was surprisingly clear and focused. They were in so deep now, she no longer cared that their plan was essentially seat-of-the-pants and technically illegal, or that a mistake was potentially lethal. Once inside, they would just have to do whatever it took to get the job done. And she was ready to do whatever it took.

She took a deep breath to help calm her runaway pulse and gripped the video camera a little tighter. After taking a quick look around to make sure no one was up and about the neighborhood, she decided the coast was clear and hurried over to where he was waiting for her.

"I'll go in first and help you up."

He slipped inside the house, and she handed the camcorder to him. He set it down and reached for her. She grabbed hold of his outstretched arms, and he easily lifted her through the window. Then they paused a moment to orient themselves.

Wade put his lips to her ear. "I think the bedrooms are probably down that hallway there," he said, his voice a barely audible whisper.

She nodded, accepting the camcorder back from him. He moved forward slowly, picking his way carefully around the shadowy lumps of furniture silhouetted by the moonlight spilling into the room through the open window. She kept one hand pressed lightly against his back for guidance as she tiptoed down the hallway behind him. The blood was pounding loudly in her ears, and she found herself taking tiny, shallow breaths as tension twisted its grip tighter and tighter around her lungs and made it increasingly difficult to breathe. Her insides were churning so violently she wondered briefly if the glass of milk she'd had with dinner had turned to butter yet.

Wade opened the first door as quietly as possible and peeked into the room. A moment later, he glanced back at her, shaking his head, and they moved toward the next door. Once again, he came up empty. The third time, however, he gave her the thumbs up signal. "Get ready," he mouthed silently, and she nodded again, grinning as a fresh shot of adrenaline-filled excitement surged through her. Move over, Bond—there's a new spy in town.

Wade stepped into the room, and a moment later, she saw the bright beam of his flashlight click on. She heard a startled yelp and then a loud thump as something solid hit the floor. Her heart skipped a beat as she wondered what on earth had happened.

"Get up," a voice snarled. She closed her eyes thankfully, and breathed a sigh of relief as she recognized Wade's voice.

It was time to jump into action. She flipped the switch on the camcorder to standby and peeked around the half-open doorway. It was dark inside the bedroom, and for a moment, all she could make out was a thin beam of light shining down toward the floor and onto a man who was shielding his eyes in protest. Then the bedside lamp clicked on.

Dave Dayner was cowering on his knees and whimpering fearfully. As the room lit up to reveal his attacker, his mouth dropped open in astonishment. "You! What are you doing here?" he gasped.

Wade reached down to grab him by the collar of his pyjama top and hauled him back up onto the bed in a sitting position, with his back facing toward the door. He then signaled Tanya with a slight nod of his head, and she clicked the record button on.

Sputtering in anger, Dave started to get up from the bed, but Wade pushed him down again with a violent shove and towered menacingly over top of him. "I think it's time you and I had a little heart to heart."

Staring at Wade through the tiny viewfinder of the camcorder, Tanya shuddered involuntarily at the intimidating picture he presented. With the shadows further darkening his murderous expression and the size of his frame literally dwarfing Dave's much slighter build, he certainly appeared one dark and dangerous adversary. Poor Dave. All the fight drained out of the man, and he seemed to wilt under the awesome force of Wade's angry presence.

"What about?" Dave asked, his tone sullen.

"Well, for starters, I'd like to continue the conversation we were having earlier today before it was interrupted by that untimely phone call. I believe we were talking about automatic weapons and CFBA."

"I'm not telling you anything."

"Oh, I know everything, Dave. You're going down big time, you hear?"

"Me? I've done nothing wrong."

"No? Well, I'd call embezzling money from Pacific Realtors to buy automatic weapons something wrong. And I'm sure the judge and jury in your court case are going to agree with me."

"You'll never prove anything," Dave shrugged. Though he was trying to project an aura of nonchalance, his twitching fingers belied his apparent lack of concern as they worried at the bed sheets.

"Oh, but we already have proof. We have photocopies of the canceled checks made out to Starbright Enterprises. And we both know who authorized payment of the phony invoices. You know, embezzlement is a serious offense, and you're going to be locked up for a long time. A pretty boy like you is going to catch the interest of quite a few of your fellow inmates. Just try not to drop the soap in the shower, if you get my drift."

"Please, don't do this to me."

Tanya grinned as she caught the genuine fear in Dave's voice. Wade's plan was working beautifully. Another threat or two like that last one and the big, nasty alley cat would soon have the helpless little canary singing like a stool pigeon.

"Give me one good reason why you shouldn't rot in a jail cell alongside Reverend White and the rest of his buddies?"

"I . . . I . . . Oh, man, you gotta give me a break. Please. I don't want to go to jail."

Wade sighed. "How the hell did you get mixed up in all this anyway, Dayner?"

"Reverend White knew I was a loyal follower, and so he approached me and asked me to help raise some money. For CFBA."

"And what is CFBA going to use the money for?"

"Campaign funds."

"Campaign funds," Wade repeated frowning, remembering what he'd heard about Reverend White wanting to run for local office. "As in political campaign?"

Dayner nodded.

"So where do the guns fit in?"

"They're part of our fund-raising strategy."

Wade frowned in confusion. "Are you telling me that you're selling guns to raise money for Reverend White's political campaign?"

"That's right. Don't worry," he added quickly in response to the look of incredulity on Wade's face. "I must admit I was a little shocked myself at first, but after the reverend explained it to me, it all made sense. Arms sales are much more profitable than simply putting our donations in the bank and letting the interest accrue. The guns aren't being sold on American soil, so they won't be responsible for any violence in this country. They're going to the Middle East where violence is such a normal way of life, it really doesn't matter. They're going to buy guns from someone, so it might as well be from us."

Tanya nearly cried out in protest at Dave's words, remembering only at the very last second hers was a covert role, and the success of their mission depended on Dave not knowing she was there. She bit back rising nausea and struggled to draw breath as the hard weight of shock pushed momentarily against her chest and threatened to squeeze all life from her inner organs. Then outrage replaced shock, and her body trembled violently in protest against the innocent victims who were going to suffer at the hands of these hypocritical creeps. A reverend selling guns to further his own political agenda? Why, it was unthinkable. She and Wade needed to stop these people!

Willing her shaking hands to hold the camcorder steady, Tanya studied Wade through the recorder lens, wondering what he was thinking. She could see the blood had drained from his face and that his fists were clenched tightly together. No doubt he was also struggling to maintain his composure.

Wade was silent for a few seconds longer, and Tanya watched as he forced a semblance of calm to his features.

"So you're selling guns to raise campaign funds for Reverend White? That's quite inventive." Wade nodded his head slowly, feigning reluctant admiration. "I'm impressed."

"Yes, and for all the other CFBA candidates," Dave told him proudly.

"So what does CFBA stand for, exactly?"

"Coalition for a Better America. We have branches all across the country to fund political candidates who support our views. Once we get more of them into office, we can start changing things."

"What kinds of things?"

"America has lost its morality, and we're going to legislate it back. We plan to introduce bills that ban immoral activities like drug and alcohol consumption, sex before marriage, same sex marriage, and practicing non-Christian religions. We'll also integrate Christian teachings into the classroom so our kids grow up knowing the difference between right and wrong and have the proper respect for God's ways. We want to increase the penalties for crime and turn prisons into work camps so criminals are properly punished for their transgressions. The three strikes rule should be mandatory in all states."

"Wow. You guys have it all figured out, don't you?"

Dave nodded vigorously. "The CFBA has been planning this for years, and now, it's all finally starting to happen. You can still join us, you know. It's not too late. Let me talk to the reverend. I'm sure we can work out our previous misunderstanding, and I know he could use a guy like you."

"I'm flattered, but I don't think I'd fit in with the rest of the group."

Dave was clearly disappointed by Wade's response. "You really should think about it," he insisted.

"Okay. I will," Wade promised. "Why don't you tell me where the guns are coming from?"

Dave frowned. "I don't think I should tell you that."

"So you want to go to jail after all? Okay, have it your way."

"Wait a minute. Are you saying that if I tell you about the guns, you'll let me go?"

"Not exactly. But I do know the FBI really wants to nail these guys. And if you tell me what I need to know, I think it's a safe bet that we can work a deal with them."

Dave stared at him in silence for a moment. "I have to think about it."

"No can do, Dayner. We already have enough to nail everyone, even without your testimony. But it would be handy to have you help us clean up some loose ends. You've got to decide right now though. Tomorrow will be too late, and once we move, you'll be going down along with everyone else."

"Okay, okay. You win."

"All right. Now what about the guns?"

"They're military surplus. Someone on the inside is sending them to us."

"Who?"

"I don't know. Look, Wade, I really don't," he insisted at Wade's disbelieving expression. "They don't tell me everything, you know."

"Okay. But what you're telling me is that you're getting the guns from someone in the US military, right? Are they selling them to you or are they part of the CFBA as well?"

Dave didn't answer.

"Don't hold out on me, Dave," Wade warned.

"CFBA," Dave responded, his tone sullen.

Wade shook his head in disgust. "Tell me something, Dave. Don't you think the CFBA is being a little hypocritical here? It doesn't sound very Christian to me to be stealing guns from one's own government and selling them overseas for personal gain."

Dave shook his head. "Not at all. We really have no choice," he explained. America is in such a mess that we need to take some drastic steps to fix her. It will all work out in the end, though."

"I see. The end justifies the means, is that it?"

"Yes. Exactly," Dave nodded vigorously in agreement. "Our mission is to end the violence and corruption that's taken over our nation and replace it with order and serenity. As soon as everyone embraces the One True Faith, we can end pain and suffering and drive out the murderers, child molesters, gays, gang members, and drug lords once and for all. Don't you see? The world will be a much better place once everything is organized properly. We can end wars, eliminate world hunger, and wipe out poverty forever. With the church in charge, everyone will be treated equally and fairly. No one will want for anything. What better justification than that?"

Wade raised one eyebrow in disbelief, and his eyes briefly met Tanya's startled ones over top the camcorder. Blood turned to ice in her veins as cold shock chilled her to the bone. Dave had obviously been listening to a few too many sermons. The man so clearly believed everything he was telling Wade that she could envision him doing anything the good reverend might tell him to do. Dave was obviously a gullible idiot, which meant he was potentially a very real danger to society. How many more Daves did Reverend White have working for him in CFBA? How many cities across America had CFBA already invaded?

"Hmmm," she heard Wade respond noncommittally. "One last question. Tell me who your inside guy is."

"What are you talking about?"

"We know that someone from the police department is working with you. Who is it?"

Dave frowned. "I really don't know. This is the first I've heard of it."

Wade eyed him doubtfully. "Well, Dayner, you're not proving to be much in the way of help. Is there anything else you can tell me so I can put in a good word for you with the FBI?"

Dave's eyes burned with fanaticism. "You can't stop us you know. It's too late. We're strong, and we're growing even stronger every day. God has given us Reverend White to ensure America will soon embrace the One True Faith. Are you sure you don't want to join us?"

"Sorry, Dayner, but you're going to have to count me out of this one. You can tell Reverend White I'd love to join his coalition, but unfortunately I have a previous commitment." He glanced down at his watch. "Well, time to run. It's been, shall we say . . . informative. The FBI will be pleased, I'm sure. Your friends, on the other hand, are going to be rather peeved when they find out you've betrayed their confidence. I suggest you take an extended holiday for the next little while before they do to you what they did to my brother-in-law."

Wade crossed his arms and looked down at Dave, his features stern and his manner extremely serious. "I'm going to leave now. I suggest you stay in your room until after I've left, because I can be extremely dangerous when I'm angry. Oh, and I highly recommend you forget about your beauty sleep and start packing."

He glanced briefly at Tanya and motioned his head in the direction of their escape route ever so slightly. She clicked off the camcorder and scooted down the hall. He joined her at the open window a moment later and took the camcorder from her, while she slipped through the window and jumped the short distance to the ground below.

He landed beside her and grabbed her hand. "Let's get out of here," he whispered, tugging urgently.

Throwing caution to the wind, they ran for the car as quickly as Tanya could move her feet. It wasn't nearly fast enough for Wade who half dragged her behind him as they raced across the street and up half a block to where they had left their vehicle. Upon reaching, it she leaned against the front fender, panting heavily as she struggled to inhale enough oxygen to fill her protesting lungs, while Wade reached into his pocket for the key fob.

"Get in," he ordered as the door locks snapped up. She wrenched open the passenger door and scrambled inside. The engine fired to life, and he tossed the camcorder into her lap before speeding away from the curb.

"We did it!" she announced gleefully once she'd managed to get her breath back.

"Yeah, we did," he acknowledged, offering a conspiratorial smile of triumph as he glanced briefly in her direction.

"Can you believe what Dave was saying? He's one sick puppy, that's for sure. I wonder how many people CFBA has recruited at this point."

"Too many." Wade's expression was grim and his tone deadly serious as he looked at her once more. "We've got to get this video to Agent Turvey as soon as possible."

Chapter Twelve

She was falling again, down into the deep, dark unknown pit of terror where unimaginable horrors awaited to swallow her up. A hurricane-force gale whistled shrilly as it whipped her helpless body back and forth across the centre of the dark void, coldly indifferent to her plaintive cries to make it stop. She reached out with both hands to grasp something, anything to bring her flailing body under control, but captured only nothingness in her empty grip.

From out of the darkness, a beacon of hope flared to life as a familiar voice called her name. She turned her head toward the sound and spied a shadowy figure reaching toward her. She stretched her arms out as far as they could go, but still they could not quite make contact. Then the man began to fall away from her, hurtling down into the black emptiness and leaving her on her own once again. She screamed his name, begging him not to leave her, but the wind howled derisively in her ears, mocking her useless attempts to call him back. The tears streamed down her cheeks as she realized he was gone forever . . .

Tanya woke, shivering at the haunting memory of the chilling images that were still so terrifyingly vivid inside her head. She'd had this same particular dream before, but tonight, it seemed different somehow. It took her a moment to realize why. Tonight, the falling body had been given a face. And that face had been Wade's.

She chewed at her lip in dismay as realization dawned on her that losing Wade was in fact a very real possibility. Tomorrow, they would hand over her recording of Wade's conversation with Dave Dayner to Agent Turvey, and once the FBI had arrested Reverend White and his band of crazy fanatics, she and Wade would no longer be fugitives. Then what?

Wade would be free to continue on with his life, but what about her? She knew next to nothing about her past. Family and friends were unknown to her, faceless shadows, all of them. Except for Wade. He had been there from her very first waking memory, and she couldn't imagine being without him. He was all she knew, and everything she wanted.

But would he want to continue being a part of her life once he had avenged his brother-in-law's death and cleared his sister's name? She reminded herself again how very little she actually knew about him. About his family, where he lived, or his goals and aspirations. Perhaps he'd already made future plans for himself that didn't include her.

An acute sense of loss wrenched at her heart, and she lifted one hand to her mouth to smother the tiny cry of pain that escaped her lips. The thought of Wade not wanting her was too much to bear. She threw back the covers and jumped up out of bed, an overwhelming need to reassure herself that he was still with her driving her into the next room.

She tiptoed toward the bed and stood over his sleeping form a few moments, watching him hungrily and wanting more than anything else at this particular moment to crawl into bed beside him. Her body ached to hold him, yearned to feel his lean, hard body locked in passionate embrace with hers.

Yet Big Brother Wade had made it quite clear that wouldn't be happening again. He'd told her he wanted no distractions while he was pursuing the bad guys because he needed to keep a clear head in order to keep her safe. Resentment flared. Was that all she was to him—a distraction? Well, she wasn't so desperate for him that she had to beg.

Or was she? She stared down at his sleeping form, her heart aching with longing as she acknowledged to herself that tonight might be the very last opportunity she would have to be intimate with him again. Dare she climb into bed beside him and ask him to make love to her one more time? Indecision gnawed at her insides as she considered how embarrassed and foolish she would feel if he refused her request. Was the possibility of his saying yes worth the risk of rejection? Or would her fear of him saying no prevent her from ever knowing for sure what his answer might have been?

Taking a deep breath, she tugged gently at the covers and slipped into the bed, slowly inching closer to his sleeping form. The sound of his slow, rhythmic breathing and the delightful tickle of his breath against her shoulder were causing that now familiar warm and fuzzy feeling to spread throughout her body. She pressed her lips against his chest, inhaling deeply of his scent, savoring both touch and taste. Being this close to him filled her with a sense of peaceful contentment, and along with it, a feeling of completeness.

Wade stirred in his sleep and slipped one arm around her to cuddle her against him. She relaxed against his body, pressing her own in closer. One finger twisted into the thick hair on his chest, and she twirled it round and round, the feel of soft curls against hard muscle a fascinating contrast. Her palm rested against his breastbone, and through it, she could feel the deep, steady beating of his pulse.

She pressed her head against his heart, sighing contentedly. Her finger moved to trace the outline of his bicep, and she marvelled again at the perfect proportioning of his masculine physique. Years of physical labor had crafted a body of magnificent beauty. A body she would never tire of admiring, or of touching. Her lips brushed his neck in a tender caress.

"Mmmm," a voice murmured softly in her ear, its deep, resonant tones vibrating gently against her skin, sending a rush of tingles down her spine. "That's a nice way to wake up."

"I'm glad you approve," she teased softly, nipping at his neck as she lightly skimmed one hand down the length of his body. "Oh! You are awake. Now, what do you propose we do about it?"

"One or two things come to mind."

"Really? Like what?"

"Like making mad, passionate love to your sexy little body."

"Mad and passionate, you say?"

"That's right. Wildly mad and extremely passionate."

"Show me," she commanded.

His hands came up to cup her face in a fiercely possessive grip, and his lips crushed into hers with savage intensity. Her own lips parted in instant submission, and with a throaty growl of triumph, he thrust his tongue deep inside her mouth. A soft cry of encouragement escaped from the back of her throat.

One arm moved across her shoulders and without breaking contact with her lips, in a single flowing motion he rolled her over onto her back and landed on top of her. Her whimper deepened to a purr of feminine satisfaction, and sighing with pleasure, she wound her arms around his neck to pull him closer. He grunted an equally satisfied reply and further intensified his assault on her senses, nipping lightly at her jaw line and then moving to the soft skin of her neck. Fire suffused her body, and she shifted restlessly beneath him.

Still kissing her, he moved his hand down the side of her body and lifted her night gown up to her neck with a single jerk. His lips moved to one breast, closing around the nipple as his teeth gently took it in his mouth. She cried out in pleasure, taking his head in her hands and

arching her back closer toward his mouth. He shifted to the other breast, offering it identical pleasure.

"Mmmmmm. Yes. Oh, yes," she encouraged.

"You mean like this? And this?" he teased.

"Oooh! Yes. Just like that," she confirmed, gasping as his tongue traced a circular pattern around her pleasure-swollen nipple.

"How about this," he asked, moving one hand to the soft curls between her legs.

"Mmmmmm," she purred. "I like that too." Her legs parted to allow him easier access.

He moved his hand over her most intimate parts, gently stimulating her there until, becoming more and more desperate for release, she cried out for him.

"You're all hot and wet for me," he observed. A smug, satisfied smile curved his lips.

"Then for Pete's sake, make love to me!"

He laughed softly. "Not yet."

"Wa-ade! Please!"

He laughed again, this time triumphantly. A moment later, he was inside and moving hard and fast against her. She clung to him desperately, crying out his name as he brought her to a quick and earth-shattering climax. He followed almost immediately and collapsed into her arms, his eyes closed, and his weight resting heavily against her as his breathing slowly returned to normal.

"Wade," she whispered softly.

"What is it?" he whispered back, eyes still closed.

"You were right."

"About what?"

"That was wildly mad and extremely passionate. Can we do it again?"

He opened one eye. "You mean . . . right now?"

"Mmm hmm. This sexy little body wants more."

The other eye opened. "Then bring that sexy little body over here," he growled, raising himself up to rest on his elbows above her.

She giggled and reached for him. He lowered his lips to hers in a slow, tender kiss that melted every inch of her body, turning her insides to quivering jelly. She relaxed back against the pillows, exulting in the marvellous sensations coursing through her.

"That's it," he encouraged. "Just relax, and let me do the work." He kissed the tip of her nose, her eyes, and then nibbled at the base of her ear before covering her face and neck with hot, wet kisses. He worked his way slowly over every inch of her body, tracing a trail of shivery heat across her burning skin, pausing to give special attention to those areas of her body that responded even more intensely to his lovemaking. By the time he had finished, she was trembling violently.

He made love to her then, sweetly, gently, encouraging her with his hands and his voice as she climaxed again and again. When at last she could bear no more, he took her in his arms and cradled her against his chest.

"This wasn't supposed to happen, you know," he murmured softly in her ear. "But I just can't seem to help myself where you're concerned."

A small smile of triumph curved her lips. "Glad to hear it," she whispered back, just before falling into a deep and restful sleep.

* * * * *

A light nibbling on one breast woke her up, and she stretched luxuriously, blinking sleepily at the owner of the magical mouth. "Mmmm. That *is* a nice way to wake up!"

They made love again, and to Tanya, it was every bit as satisfying as the night before. It was not until she lay cuddled against him, satiated and content and contemplating the possibility of spending the entire day in bed with Wade that she remembered the day's task ahead of them. They were to contact Agent Turvey and hand over their video evidence to him. Then it would be only a matter of time before they could come out of their forced hiding. The thought made her recall her fears of the night before, and she wondered again what sort of future she and Wade might have.

He must want them to be together. How could he not, after making such passionate yet tender love to her last night and again this morning? Just now he had been the most gentle lover imaginable. He had touched her like a priceless treasure. Worshipped her body with his mouth and hands. Even through the passion of his own release, he had continued to hold her carefully, almost reverently in his arms. And now, after the loving was all done, he was cradling her tenderly to his heart as if she were the most precious thing in all the world to him. He made her feel special. Cherished. Loved.

At that moment, she wished Agent Turvey had never tracked them down and taken them into his confidence. Without Agent Turvey, they would have been forced to stay in hiding together a while longer. Alone together, just the two of them. It would have provided a little more time to make Wade fall in love with her, just as she suspected she herself was doing with him.

She certainly cared about him deeply. Perhaps a little too deeply, given how little she really knew about him. Or about her own life, for that matter. And because she did care so much, she was now faced with another worry. Reverend White's upcoming trial.

She had little doubt that she and Wade would be called upon to testify against the man and his followers. However, after listening to Dan Dayner's ranting last night about the righteous cause of the Church of the One True Faith, she also suspected it very likely that some of his more faithful fanatics would try doing whatever they could to free their beloved leader. Like perhaps killing the Crown witnesses?

Should Agent Turvey offer them the option of not testifying, she would seriously consider trying to talk Wade into taking it. After all they had been through, she was tired of hiding, of looking over her shoulder every time they left the condo. She would be more than willing to disappear for a while until the trial had concluded and the men who wanted her dead were locked up safely behind bars. And she certainly had no desire to see Wade risk his life any further than he had done already. But Wade was so determined to put his brother-in-law's murderers away for good she knew he would risk vigilante gunfire in order to help ensure a guilty verdict.

Not surprisingly, then, she wasn't looking forward to their meeting with Agent Turvey and all the future consequences that could possibly stem from it. An ominous sense of foreboding came over her, and her muscles tensed as she wondered uneasily exactly what sort of future events today's meeting would put into motion.

Wade may have been thinking the same thing, for he stirred restlessly and got up from the bed. She admired again the shape of him as he walked naked toward the bathroom, her eyes drinking him in hungrily, committing each shapely curve of his incredible profile to memory as if this sight of him might be her last. The back of her neck prickled uncomfortably once he disappeared around the corner, and she couldn't seem to shake the awful feeling that things would not go well for the two of them today.

The bathroom door closed, and she lay her head back against the pillows, wishing Wade would forget about Agent Turvey for the time being and come back to bed with her. Why couldn't they let the FBI take care of things on their own? Why must Wade continually risk his life to do their job for them? And her life as well, for she wasn't about to let Wade out of her sight. One didn't let a catch like him out of the house unsupervised when she wasn't quite sure where she stood with him. In her uncertain future at least one thing was for sure—no other woman was going to get her meat hooks into Wade while she was around. Now if only she could be as confident that Wade felt the same about her.

There was a light thump at the end of the bed, and she looked up to see Charlie sitting there, watching her hopefully. When her head moved, he let out a tiny meow of greeting and came up beside her, purring loudly. She sat up and gave him an affectionate hug. "At least you're not going anywhere, my sweet baby," she whispered into his soft fur.

The bathroom door opened, and she sighed with disappointment as a few seconds later, she heard Wade rustling about in the kitchen. Resigned to the fact it was time to get up, she threw back the covers and jumped out of bed, hoping she would feel a bit more optimistic after a shower and maybe a cup of coffee.

A hot shower did improve her mood somewhat, so that she was in a slightly more positive frame of mind upon joining Wade in the kitchen.

"I'll take a shower, and then we'll take a drive out of the neighborhood before calling Agent Turvey," he advised as he handed her a cup of coffee. "I still don't want to chance our cell signal being traced here."

Her spirits plummeted at his matter-of-fact, businesslike tone. Already focused, no fixated, on nailing the bad guys, he didn't even have so much as a smile of greeting for her. It seemed all he cared about was bringing Cliff Peterson's killers to justice. Even after a night of intimate sharing and dynamite lovemaking he was already more interested in catching crooks than in sharing conversation over a cup of coffee with her.

"Once we give the video to Turvey, we'll lie low and wait for him to make the arrests," he continued. "Once I know for sure who killed Cliff and my sister is released from jail, our lives should get back to normal."

"Great. Sounds like a plan to me," she enthused weakly, wondering exactly what he meant by "normal." Normal as in the two of them continuing to be together as they had over the past week, or normal as in before her accident and resulting amnesia? Unfortunately, she had absolutely no idea what normal was prior to her fall. "Just what the hell is normal?" she wanted to scream at him in frustration.

Some of her inner turmoil must have shown in her face, for he paused a moment, looking at her uncertainly. "Is something the matter?"

"No . . . not really," she responded hesitantly.

"What do you mean, not really?"

She stared at him unhappily, biting her bottom lip with indecision. The question had been weighing on her mind for some time now, and here was a perfect opportunity to bring the matter up for discussion. She took a deep breath and opened her mouth again before she could chicken out. "Well, I was just wondering . . . what about us?"

Wade stared down into her anxious eyes, twin blades of guilt and indecision twisting razor sharp in his gut. All along, he had known that the moment of truth was inevitable, but for the past week, he had been putting off coming clean about the nature of their prior relationship. He was not looking forward to the consequences of telling her the truth, which was that he had deliberately taken advantage of her amnesia in order to find out everything he could about the people responsible for Cliff's death and his sister's wrongful incarceration.

At least, that had been his original intention. But somewhere along the way things had changed, and life had gotten a lot more complicated. Ever since he and Tanya had stopped fighting long enough to be civil to one another, his attitude toward her had shifted a one-hundred-and-eighty-degree curve in the opposite direction, so that now he found himself greatly admiring the same impulsive, in-your-face attitude he had previously loathed. And despite his best efforts to avoid it, their mutual attraction had worn down his steadily weakening defenses until mortal enemies had become intimate. But though his feelings toward her had changed, what was she going to think of him when the truth was finally out in the open? A week ago, he couldn't have cared less, but it did matter now. In fact, it now mattered very much.

"What about us?" he asked cautiously, hating himself for being such a coward, especially when he saw her eyes darken with pain and hurt.

His hesitation was a pretty good indication of how he felt, Tanya realized, her heart sinking with disappointment as the fragile hope drained out of her. She swallowed hard, finding it difficult to breathe. It seemed Wade did not feel the same way she did after all. For if he had, surely he would not be looking as if at this particular moment he would rather be tossed blind folded into a pit of rattlesnakes than look her in the face. Still, though it was going to hurt, she had to hear him say the words. "After this is over . . . is there going to be an us?"

He looked even more miserable than ever as he took her hand and held it awkwardly between his palms. "Tanya, as soon as this is all over, we need to have a serious talk. About us."

She nodded, unable to say anything, fearing her voice would crack and betray just how close to tears she was. And pride was all she had left, since she had just lost everything else in her life that really mattered. Her hopes, her dreams, and her chance at love. For after being with Wade, she knew no one else could ever fill the empty void his leaving was going to carve deep into her heart. But if she couldn't stop him from going, when the time came, she would hold her head up as he said goodbye, so that he would remember her smile instead of her tears and never guess at the depth of her heartache.

Pride alone forced her to endure his searching glance and accept the comforting squeeze of his hand without flinching. Could he possibly

look any more relieved that she wasn't going to get upset with him? she wondered bitterly.

"I'll grab a quick shower, and then we can get going."

He disappeared around the corner, and she was left standing by herself, still holding onto the cup of coffee he had given her. She looked down at it and grimaced, a wave of nausea washing over her as the smell finally registered. Down the sink it went. She considered getting herself a bowl of cereal and immediately thought better of it when her stomach again tightened in protest. It was simply not up to handling food of any sort at the moment.

She sat quietly at the kitchen table as she waited for Wade to finish getting ready. It rather surprised her that the pain didn't hurt nearly as much as she would have expected, but she supposed she was still blessedly numb with shock at the realization that she truly was going to lose him forever. No doubt that would wear off soon enough, but at least it might help get her through the meeting with Agent Turvey and perhaps even the rest of the day.

It didn't take Wade long to shower and dress, and very soon, they were on their way, their video evidence tucked safely away in Tanya's purse. Wade drove away from their neighborhood, ever cautious about the possibility of the call being traced. Eventually, he pulled over, made the call to the FBI agent and turned his phone off again.

"What did he say?" she asked as he tucked the phone back into his pocket.

"He was glad to hear from us, and very impressed with what we have on video. He wants to meet with us right away."

"That's great," she told him, trying to sound genuinely enthusiastic. But it was difficult to be excited about a meeting that was going to bring her one step closer to her final parting with Wade. "Where?"

"At the Hilton on Sixth Avenue. In the lobby. At noon."

She glanced down at her watch. It was just after ten. "We've got some time. What do you want to do?"

He shrugged. "We might as well head over there now. You can grab something to eat in the hotel restaurant while we're waiting. I noticed you never ate breakfast."

"Wasn't really hungry," she mumbled.

It took them twenty minutes to drive to the Hilton and another five or so to park and walk across the lot and into the hotel. The restaurant was relatively empty, and at Wade's request, the host led them over to a table by the window. It gave them a good view of the hotel entrance and city street outside, as well as a clear line of sight into the lobby.

Tanya picked up one of the menus the woman had left on the table. Though she still wasn't feeling particularly hungry, she figured she might as well order something. It would at least help pass the time while they were waiting for Agent Turvey to arrive. It would also give her something to focus on other than the person sitting across the table from her. Neither had said much to the other since their conversation this morning, and the resulting silence between them was becoming increasingly strained.

The waitress came by, and Tanya ordered a ham and cheese croissant, gritting her teeth when the woman instantly responded to Wade's friendly smile as he requested a coffee. Did the man have to be quite so charming to every female he met, she wondered jealously. She saw Wade's eyes narrow as he intercepted her evil glare at the waitress. He gave her an inquisitive look once the woman had left the table, but pride stayed her tongue, and she deliberately looked away.

Staring out the window, she searched for some distraction to relieve the tension that was building inside her and winding the knots in her stomach tighter and tighter with each passing moment. A man washing the windows of the office building across the street caught her attention, and she watched absently as he swished the handle of his foam covered blade back and forth and then followed up with the rubber scraper on the reverse side.

The maintenance worker finished drying the window in front of him and began lowering his scaffold one floor down. Without warning, the line on one end of the platform gave way and the bottom collapsed, swinging crazily into space as the free end dropped toward the ground. Tanya watched in horror as the man lost his footing and began to fall. She closed her eyes in denial, thus failing to realize that a safety line attached him to the scaffold so that he fell only a few feet.

"Daddy," she screamed, her voice a high-pitched wail of sheer terror, and suddenly, it all came flooding back. Her father's smiling face, his lightly teasing banter, and his laughter as he hugged his little girl goodbye before heading off to work. The accidental fall and his resulting death. The shock. The pain. The anguish. The heartbreak of both her and her mother. The anger at the people responsible . . .

"You!" she gasped, opening her eyes to stare at Wade in disbelief. "You . . . you . . . " Words failed her as shock rendered her temporarily speechless, and she could only gape helplessly at the man across the table from her. The man whose family had ruined hers. The man whose family she'd vowed would pay for killing her father. "You swine!" she finally managed to sputter at him.

"Tanya, wait," he told her as he reached for one of her hands. "Please, let me explain."

She snatched her hand back from the table, her eyes spitting twin daggers of hate into his. "Forget it, you sneaky bastard. I'm not interested in hearing any explanation from you. It's very clear to me this is some kind of sick revenge on your part."

Cold anger replaced shock as the truth behind his deception hit home. It was obvious he had lured her into bed, pretending to care for her as he exacted payback for the way she had treated him in high school and then set out to ruin his father's business upon graduation. Well, he should be thankful that was all she ever did to him. His family certainly deserved a lot worse. But she? What had she ever done to deserve this, besides give up to those butchers the single most important person in her life? Her biggest and greatest hero. The father she had worshipped and idolized.

To be made a fool of was bad enough, but the knowledge that he had made her truly care for him fired her with an even greater anger. She threw her water glass at him. "How could you do this to me?"

Wade slapped the glass aside, sending a spray of water through the air and over toward the next table. It landed with a muffled thump on the carpet, some of it splashing up onto the bare legs of the young woman sitting there who shrieked in surprise at the unexpected cold on her skin. Her partner spun in his seat to glare at Wade in angry indignation. "Hey, buddy. What the hell are you doing?"

Tanya swiveled around to glare at the man. "Butt out, mister," she warned. "Can't you see this is a private conversation. Besides, I have first dibs on his hide." She picked up Wade's water glass, which was still half full, and waved it menacingly in his direction.

Wade glanced briefly around the room, noting that it was beginning to fill, and people were beginning to stare in their direction, openly curious about the ruckus they were creating. "Tanya, calm down."

"Calm down? Calm down?" she repeated, her voice rising to a high-pitched squeak of indignation. "You people killed my father, and now you have the nerve to tell me to calm down?"

"Bloody hell, Tanya," he shouted back, finally losing patience. "For the last time, I am not personally responsible for the death of your father. And neither is my family's company."

"Don't give me that. Your faulty equipment caused his death. And if your father had maintained it properly, my father would still be alive today."

"That's bull shit. There was absolutely nothing wrong with the equipment. If your father hadn't been drinking, he wouldn't have been so careless."

She stared at him, shocked beyond belief at the audacity of his lie. "Liar! How dare you malign the memory of my father!"

"I'm not lying, Tanya. Your father was impaired when he went up on that ledge, and he should have known better. It was fortunate he didn't take out any of his crew working on the floor beneath him when he fell." His anger died on the spot as he realized this piece of information was indeed news to her. "You really didn't know, did you?" he whispered in a soft tone.

She shook her head, refusing to be fooled by the false sincerity in his eyes or the feigned sympathy in his voice. "I don't believe you," she challenged.

"It's true. It was your parents' anniversary that day, and your mother came by to bring your father a special, home-cooked lunch. She opened a bottle of champagne, but he should have known better than to drink it with her. I guess he didn't want to disappoint your mother."

She stared at him uncertainly. Her father had indeed died on her parents' fifteenth wedding anniversary, but she'd never been told anything about a special anniversary lunch. Could it possibly be true? Had her mother deliberately kept this information from her, perhaps concocting a fictitious story of faulty equipment to assuage her guilty conscience and conceal her partial responsibility for the death of her husband? It seemed inconceivable that her mother would condone, even encourage, Tanya's determination all these past years to make Able Construction pay for something that wasn't even their fault. She shook her head. "I don't believe you," she replied, but she knew her voice lacked conviction.

"It's true," he repeated. "I wouldn't lie about something like that." He watched the conflicting emotions dance across her troubled features. Disbelief, disillusionment, denial, and finally, a tentative acceptance of the possibility that he might be telling the truth. "You really believed my father was at fault, didn't you. I can see now why you've had it in for his company all these years. I'm glad it wasn't me personally," he added with a mischievous grin, hoping to lighten her mood somewhat.

One eyebrow raised as she gave him a disgusted look. He must be joking. Not personal? Oh, it was very personal. "If you're so innocent, mister, then how come you had me fired from the city?"

"What?" He stared at her in renewed exasperation. "Listen, Tanya, you got yourself fired. You went out of your way to harass me once I took over from my father. What with your ridiculous requests, your deliberate delay tactics and resulting fines, I was having so many problems in obtaining the permits necessary to operate my business that I had to complain. Otherwise, if you'd had your way, I'd be out of business by now."

"Yeah, well that was the plan. Too bad I never succeeded. But you didn't have to go and make a fool out of me over it. Wasn't the fact that I was fired satisfaction enough for you?"

He frowned. "What do you mean?"

She rolled her eyes and sighed heavily. "Oh, please. You know very well I'm talking about the fact that you've been being so nice to me just so I would sleep with you so you could throw it all back in my face when my memory returned. Well, that was a low blow, Wade, even for a snake like you."

"It wasn't like that, Tanya. I swear."

But she had stopped listening, for the added shock and pain of her mother's betrayal on top of Wade's had moved her far beyond the ability to hear his words or to recognize the sincerity behind them.

"You used me, Wade. But the fun's over. I'm onto you now, and I never want to see you again. You hear me? Never!" She leaped to her feet. "Stay away from me. I'm warning you." That said, she raced out of the restaurant.

Wade almost groaned aloud as he watched her leave, acknowledging to himself that he had really blown it this morning by not being honest about his feelings toward her. But whether it would have made any difference to her reaction just now he would never know, for she would most probably never give him a chance to explain.

If only she weren't so impulsive and hotheaded, so quick to anger and even quicker to react without thinking things through. For if she had stopped to think about it, she would have realized that no man made love to a woman the way he'd done to her without caring very deeply for his partner. He was sorely tempted to go after her and shake some sense into that messed-up little head of hers before she went and did anything foolish.

Such as end up in the evil clutches of Reverend White. Alarm bells went off in his head, causing him to leap immediately to his feet. In the state she was in, the last thing on her mind would be avoiding the Church of the One True Faith gang. She could be in grave danger this very moment, and it was his own stupidity which had put her there.

He fumbled for his wallet and tossed some bills down onto the table, mumbling an apology to the surprised waitress who chose at that moment to appear with Tanya's sandwich. He then rushed out into the main lobby of the hotel and looked around for Tanya. She was nowhere in sight.

He stepped outside and saw her talking to Agent Turvey beside a car parked at the curb. Even as he began to move forward, Turvey held open the passenger door, and Tanya climbed in. Wade stopped, deciding it best to let her go.

Common sense dictated it was the right thing to do. She would be safer with the FBI agent than with him. And no doubt happier. Once this terrible ordeal was over, she would be free to pick up the pieces of her life, put her past behind her and move on. As for himself? Well, he should have known no good could have come from falling for a woman who hated his guts.

He watched as the car inched away from the curb, his heart bleak, and wishing things could be different between them. But any last remaining vestiges of hope were dashed as Tanya held her middle finger up to the window, deliberately keeping her face turned away from him.

He noticed someone sitting in the backseat and squinted his eyes for a better view. The man looked vaguely familiar, and Wade struggled for a second or two to place him.

"Damn!" He swore so violently that a woman passing by him on the sidewalk nearly jumped out of her skin. She eyed him warily and gave him a wide berth, but Wade never noticed. He instead watched helplessly as the car disappeared up the street. His heart leaped to his throat, and for a brief moment, he thought he would be physically sick, for the man in backseat was the person who had tried to chloroform Tanya at the hospital.

Chapter Thirteen

"I can't believe I was ever civil to that jerk," Tanya said to Agent Turvey with a haughty toss of her head and an angry sniff, completely ignoring for the moment the stranger sitting in the seat behind her.

The FBI agent glanced over at her. "How come?"

"Let's suffice it to say he's a sneaky, conniving little rat, plus a dirty, rotten scoundrel to boot. And I never want to see him again."

"Sounds like you two had a falling out. You seemed on pretty good terms last time I saw you guys together."

"Yeah, but that was before I knew who he was. You see, my memory's returned. Now I know all about him. Every scheming, calculating inch of his miserable hide."

"I see. Well, I'm sorry to hear that, because unfortunately, I still need to speak with him. Can you tell me where I might be able to get hold of him?"

"What for?" she shrugged. "I can tell you everything you need to know. Besides, I've got the video. Here, in my purse."

"That's all I wanted to know," Turvey assured her.

Before she knew what was happening, a hand snaked out from behind to grip her by the throat and press her back against the headrest. She gasped in surprise and began to struggle, but her supply of oxygen was dwindling rapidly, draining her strength along with it. She stopped moving, eyes silently communicating her shock and devastation at this unexpected betrayal.

Turvey pulled into a deserted alley and stopped the vehicle. His smile was pitiless as he turned toward her. "I thank you for your cooperation,

Ms. Riverton. Now, let's finish the job you started in the hospital," he ordered the other man. "She's caused us enough headaches already."

"In the glove box," the other man replied.

Turvey reached over to open the glove compartment. He pulled out a dirty rag and a glass bottle filled with clear liquid. He opened the bottle and dumped some of the liquid out onto the rag. He then anchored the bottle between his knees and leaned toward her. Her eyes bulged with horror as the rag moved closer and closer to her face.

"This won't hurt a bit," Turvey assured her just as the cloth made contact.

She began to choke as a sickly sweet odor assailed her nostrils and burned all the way down her throat and into her lungs. A wave of dizziness overcame her, and the last thing she saw before everything went black was Turvey's evil grin leering down at her.

* * * * *

Tanya awoke with a pounding headache. She lifted her head and opened her eyes, blinking them shut quickly again as the light filtering through her eyelashes bit deeply and painfully into her skull. She licked her parched lips, noting her tongue felt double its normal size. She tried to lift one hand to massage her throbbing temples, but nothing happened.

Surprised, she opened her eyes again and saw that she was alone in one corner of a large, empty room, tied to a chair, her arms strapped at her sides, and her feet roped tightly to the chair's legs. A desk was nearby, and from the top of it a light was shining in her direction. Other than that, the room was in darkness. A sick sensation of fear overcame her as she remembered what had happened.

Agent Turvey was one of the bad guys, and he now held her captive. She wondered how long she had been unconscious, and why she was still alive. After all, he now had the video in his possession. Why keep her around? Why not just get rid of her like they had with Cliff Peterson?

It was fortunate she and Wade had thought to make a copy of the video. At least, Wade would be able to give it to the local police, who could use it to move in on Reverend White and the rest of this bunch of crooked creeps. Jansen must have suspected Turvey all along, or why else would he have interfered at the mall where Wade's truck had been blown up and again when she and Wade had been stopped by Turvey outside of Reverend White's mansion? Jansen had been trying to protect them, but neither she nor Wade had realized it at the time.

But Wade didn't know which side of justice Turvey was on! Her heart skipped a beat as she realized he wouldn't go to the police, because he still suspected detective Jansen or perhaps someone else on the local force was Reverend White's contact on the inside. He would probably assume she was now under FBI protection and therefore safe from harm. Hence, he would lie low and wait to hear from Agent Turvey.

And then she understood why she was still alive. They needed her to tell them how they could get hold of Wade and perhaps even to convince him to come to them.

She thought of Wade, wishing he were here beside her right now. Then she wouldn't be quite so scared. She was never afraid when he was around. Well, not much anyway. The reassuring presence of his steady strength was always enough to calm her fears in the face of danger.

Now that she was alone and far away from the shelter of Wade's protective arms, she asked herself why she'd been so angry with him when her memory initially returned. Why had she been so quick to judge him guilty of deceiving her and so determined to push him from her life without stopping to listen to his explanation, to consider his side of the story? Out of the misty fog of her confused and chaotic thoughts, a sharp little voice of clarity whispered the answer to her. It had been fear.

Fear that Wade had stayed with her not because he cared, but rather out of a gentlemanly sense of duty to protect her from their mutual foe. Fear that his desire for her might only be physical. Fear that he didn't love her nearly as much as she loved him.

Now that she'd had a chance to think about it, she realized just how badly she'd misjudged him. Her pride, coupled with emotional baggage created and fed by years of hate, had colored her thinking. If what he told her had been true about the reason for her father's senseless death, she had done him a terrible wrong all these years. From the cold snubs and childish pranks in high school to the lost paperwork and late filing charges on his building permit applications, she had certainly done everything in her power to make him suffer needlessly. So if anyone had the right to be angry, it was him, not her. For it was she who had been the terrible monster, not him, and not his family's company.

She felt bitterly ashamed of her past behavior and intensely sorry that she would never get the opportunity to apologize for it. In the time she'd spent with Wade these past days, getting to know him without the hindering bias of her previous misconceptions, she had discovered him to be a most gentle and caring person. Thoughtful and considerate. Personable and charming. Full of calm resourcefulness and guided by a deep sense of personal honor. And to top it off, gifted with a great sense of humor. He always knew how to make her smile, even during her worst moments.

A single tear rolled down one cheek. That she had been misinformed was no excuse for the aggravation she had created for him for so many years. He certainly hadn't deserved it. Even if his father's company had been responsible for her own father's death, she had been wrong to take it out on Wade. The bizarre logic of a shattered little girl had twisted an unfortunate accident into a vendetta of hate and revenge. Too bad it was too late for her to make retribution.

A murmur of voices reached her ears, and the sound of approaching footsteps echoed in the open space of the empty room. She surmised Agent Turvey was returning to pry Wade's whereabouts from her. Well, he could torture her all he wanted, but she would die first before divulging that information. It was the least she could do for Wade.

She wrestled briefly with her bonds, knowing it was useless and hating how helpless it was making her feel. The voices grew louder, and she braced herself, not knowing quite what to expect, but preparing for the worst. The crazy thought struck her that this was just like a scene out of a James Bond movie, and she wondered how much torture 007 might be able to withstand before he passed out from the pain.

Agent Turvey and two other men came into view. One of them was the same individual who had held her against the car seat while Turvey chloroformed her.

"Well, well. The lady's finally awake. Okay, Ms. Riverton, let's get down to business, shall we? Tell us where Wade Scott is and we'll let you die quickly and painlessly."

"Get stuffed," she sniffed.

Turvey reached forward and slapped her across the face. Hard. She gasped in surprise and bit down on her bottom lip to prevent herself from crying out in pain.

"One more time, Ms. Riverton. Where is Scott?"

Tanya shuddered at the cold, ugly sound of Turvey's voice but remained silent. Her eyes flashed defiantly as she stared him down, using her anger and hate to buoy up her shaking insides. James Bond would never break under pressure, and so neither would she, she promised herself.

Turvey shook his head sadly, sighing as he did so. "Come on, Ms. Riverton. Tanya. You're making it that much harder on yourself. You know that, don't you? You told me Scott was a sneaky rat and a dirty scoundrel. So what do you care what happens to him?"

"Wade Scott is one thousand times the man you are. He's kind and gentle and honorable, while you, you're pond scum."

The man she didn't recognize hooted with laughter.

"Shut up, Bishop," Turvey scowled. He turned his attention back to Tanya. "Scott's smart, I'll give him that. He's done some pretty good detective work. That's why I need to know if he has another copy of the video I just saw."

"Of course he does," she told him sweetly. "And you can bet he's already given it to the police. So you might as well give up. You're not going to get away with this. Like you said, Wade's a smart man."

Turvey snorted. "Nice bluff, but it's not going to work. You're forgetting he already told me he suspects a leak on the local force, so I know there's no way he's going to turn over that video to anyone there. And since he has no idea of my involvement with White, all I have to do is call Scott in, and he's mine."

"I don't think so. He saw you kidnap me in front of the hotel. There's no way you'll be able to convince him to come anywhere near you."

Turvey raised an eyebrow. "Oh, come now. It hardly looked that way from where he was standing. You weren't exactly screaming out the window for help. And what about the finger you gave him as we pulled away from the curb?"

"Oh that," she shrugged. "It was our secret code. I told him I was with a couple of assholes."

Bishop laughed again. Turvey's eyes narrowed angrily, and he grasped her chin tightly with one hand, squeezing his fingers together in a viselike grip. She winced at the pain but refused to give him the satisfaction of crying out.

"That's pretty tough talk, little girl. Bet you won't be so lippy when I bring Scott in."

"You won't get him."

"Looks like he already has," Bishop remarked mildly.

Turvey spun around, and Tanya strained to see past him. She heard Turvey's bark of triumph, and her heart sank as she spied Wade's familiar form walking toward them, his hands on top of his head. Her heart leaped into her throat as she spotted the gun pressed against the small of his back.

"I caught him snooping around outside, boss."

"Good work, Billy," Bishop told him.

Tanya, on the other hand, was not impressed. What on earth was that stupid idiot doing, risking his own neck to save hers? "What the hell are you doing here, Wade?" she accused. "Of all the dumb, ridiculous stunts—"

"Shut up, Tanya," Wade growled. The last thing he needed was her sharp tongue needling him when he was trying desperately to think of a plan to save her. He suspected Turvey was packing, but couldn't tell by looking at the other two men whether they had guns concealed beneath their clothing or not. That made at least two guns he had to deal with, possibly more. He glanced quickly at Turvey's companions, noting the scarred knuckles on both men's hands. They each had obviously seen a great deal of combat and knew how to take care of themselves in a fight. The man Billy had called "boss" looked as if his nose had been broken once or twice. Judging by the cool arrogance of his manner, that one appeared to be a real scrapper.

"Well, well. If it isn't the boyfriend come to save the fair damsel in distress. Thanks, Scott. You've just saved me a great deal of trouble looking for you. Now I can just kill the two of you and get it over and done with."

"I don't think the cops would like that too much. In fact, they're surrounding the place now. It's over, Turvey. So why don't you give it up before you get hurt."

The other men glanced at about them in alarm, but Turvey only snorted his disbelief. "Relax. He's bluffing," he told the others. He reached inside his jacket and withdrew his gun, pointing it directly at Wade. "But just to be on the safe side, why don't you have a look around, Billy? I'll take it from here."

Billy glanced at Bishop, who nodded slightly. Billy withdrew his gun from Wade's back and exited the room.

Wade glanced past Turvey to focus anxiously on Tanya's pale face. Anger spurted through him as he noted the way her bindings were cutting into the soft skin on her arms. He hoped the circulation was still moving through them. "Are you all right, sweetheart?" he asked, his tone softening as he gave her a reassuring smile.

She nodded and offered him a rather weak smile in return. "What are you doing here, Wade?"

"Looking for you."

"Why?"

"Because I love you." There, he had finally admitted it to her. If they were both going to die, at least he would go knowing he'd told her how he felt.

"You do?"

"Yeah, I do. And I would have told you that in the restaurant if you'd stopped yelling at me long enough to listen."

She made a face. "Sorry about that. And I'm sorry I got you into this mess. I love you too, you know."

Turvey spoke up before either of them could say anything further. "Sorry to call an end to true confession time, lovebirds, but time is running short."

"Don't you dare hurt him," Tanya warned Turvey.

Still pointing his gun at Wade, Turvey reached over and slapped her face again. "Don't tell me what to do, bitch."

Wade balled his two hands into fists and started forward. Turvey cocked the hammer of his pistol, causing Wade to check his forward movement.

"Easy, Prince Charming," Turvey warned.

"Do that to me again, and I'll bite your hand off."

Turvey laughed, an ugly sound. "It's going to bring me a great deal of pleasure to shut your nasty little mouth permanently. But first things first." His eyes narrowed menacingly as he studied Wade's expression, as if measuring the fortitude of his mettle. "Tell me what I need to know, Scott. Who else knows about the video?"

"Go to hell."

Turvey shrugged. "All right. Maybe a bullet in the leg will make you change your mind."

A shot rang out, and Wade snapped his eyes shut, bracing himself for the pain. It never came, and the agonized yelp which echoed eerily across the warehouse floor was not his own. Surprised, he opened his eyes to see Turvey cradling his bleeding hand protectively against his chest.

Wade barely hesitated before leaping for Bishop and knocking him down with a solid blow to the side of the chin. He followed up with a hard kick to the side of the head and then turned to the other man, the one he recognized from the hospital.

The two men squared off, eyeing each other in silence as each attempted to ascertain the degree of threat the other presented. The man from the hospital bared his teeth in a vicious snarl as he reached down with one hand to whip a knife from the back of his boot. Wade eyed the razor-sharp edge of the steel blade with considerable misgivings, shifting his weight to his toes for quicker maneuverability. Judging by the way his opponent was holding the knife, he was no stranger on how to use it.

The man lunged forward, and Wade retreated unscathed. The second time he wasn't so lucky, however, and the blade slashed down through his leather jacket and into the flesh of his upper arm. A sharp biting pain was followed by the sensation of sticky warmth trailing down the length of his arm.

Somewhere in the back of his mind, he vaguely heard Tanya's scream, but then nothing else registered as he forced all his powers of concentration onto the task of staying alive. The red stain on the tip of the blade was slightly mesmerizing as it wove a figure 8 pattern in the air in front of him, and with an effort, he forced his attention from the knife and onto the eyes of the man holding it.

His opponent tensed as if ready to strike a third time, but then his body relaxed, and he lowered the knife. Wade eyed him suspiciously, wondering what sort of underhanded trick the man was about to pull on him.

"Drop it," a voice from behind ordered, the commanding edge to it almost as sharp as the blade that tumbled obediently to the floor. "Now back up slowly, and put your hands on top your head."

Wade turned, sighing with heartfelt relief. "About time you showed up, Jansen."

"Hey, Scott. Mind if I join the party?" The detective grinned at him briefly over the barrel of two guns, one which was pointed at Turvey and the other at the man who was now minus the knife. "Do me a favor. Grab the cuffs out of my back pocket and toss them to your friend over there."

"Sure thing." Wade lifted the back of Jansen's jacket and spied the handcuffs tucked into one of the rear pockets of his pants. He retrieved them and slid them along the floor to the man from the hospital.

"Put them on," Jansen ordered. "Don't give me an excuse to shoot," he added when the man hesitated.

The man picked up the cuffs and slid one hand into each of the bracelets, glaring daggers at Wade as he did so. Wade breathed a sigh of relief and allowed himself to relax slightly as he heard the locking mechanisms close over both wrists.

The sound of multiple footsteps outside caused Wade to glance at the detective in alarm, but Jansen was unconcerned.

"That should be my backup. We're over here, guys," he shouted.

Several officers came into view, their guns drawn and ready. Two of them pointed their guns directly at Wade, staring at him menacingly. He froze in position and then slowly raised his hands.

"Wait! He's a good guy," Tanya called out in alarm.

"Relax, boys, he's with me."

The officers lowered their weapons, and Wade sighed again in relief. This hand-raising thing was starting to become a habit he would be only too happy to break. He reached down to pick up the discarded knife and wiped the blade on the side of his jeans before walking over to free Tanya with it.

He sliced through the ropes around her arms and upper body first. The moment she was free, she threw her arms around his neck and hugged herself to him, refusing to let go as he squatted down to cut through the bonds that held her ankles and feet captive against the chair legs.

He set the knife on the floor and stood up to gather her in his arms. "Are you all right, sweetheart?" he asked anxiously.

She looked up at him, two fat tears sliding down her cheeks as she nodded her head. "But I was so s-scared," she whispered miserably, her body beginning to tremble violently as reaction set in.

"Hush, now. Everything's going to be all right. I promise." He hugged her tighter to him for reassurance, wincing at the unexpected pain caused by material rubbing on raw flesh.

"Your arm," she cried out. "Let me see."

"It's nothing," he began, but then gave in as she started tugging with stubborn determination on the sleeve of his jacket.

"Oh my god! Look at all the blood! We need to get you to a hospital. Detective Jansen, call an ambulance for Wade right away," she ordered. "He's bleeding to death."

One of the officers came over to check out Wade's arm, ripping apart Wade's shirtsleeve so he could take a better look. "It's nothing serious, ma'am," he assured her after examining the cut. "Just a flesh wound. It'll require a couple of stitches and a tetanus shot, but he's going to be fine. I'll wrap his shirtsleeve around it to stop the blood flow, and then we'll get him to the hospital."

The officer finished tying the makeshift bandage. Jansen called for the man to join him, and he excused himself, leaving Tanya and Wade alone for the moment. They stared at each other awkwardly, neither knowing what to say. All of a sudden Tanya burst into tears.

"Oh, Wade. I'm so sorry. I nearly got us both killed. Can you ever forgive me?"

He hugged her close to him again. "Don't cry, my darling. I already have."

She pulled back and offered him a watery smile. "Really?"

"Really," he assured her. "But you know, I nearly had a heart attack when I recognized the man who tried to chloroform you at the hospital in the backseat of Turvey's car and realized that Turvey was in on it all along. I thought I'd lost you for sure. I had no idea where they'd taken you. The Starbright warehouse was the only place I could think of, and so I took a gamble and came here."

"Well, I'm glad you did." She sighed deeply. "If only I hadn't run out of that restaurant in anger. I promise I'll never do anything like it again," she announced dramatically.

Wade burst out laughing. "Until next time. Tanya, darling, don't go making promises you won't be able to keep. You're impulsive by nature, my dear. It's in your blood to act first and regret later."

She started to get huffy and then grinned at the truth of his words. "I suppose you're right."

Jansen walked over to them. "How's the arm, Scott?"

"It's nothing serious, just a flesh wound. Thanks again, Jansen."

"How did you know where we were, Detective?" Tanya asked curiously.

"When I realized Turvey was the 'guy on the inside,' I immediately called Jansen," Wade explained.

"Well, thank you for saving me, Detective Jansen. And Wade, as well," she added. "I'm sorry I've been so nasty to you."

"No problem, Ms. Riverton. All in a day's work."

"Oh please, call me Tanya. I think saving my life puts us on a first-name basis, don't you?"

Jansen acknowledged her words with a brief nod of his head. "You're going to be all right, Scott?"

Wade nodded. Just then, one of the other officers called over to Jansen and gave him a thumbs-up signal. The detective turned back to Wade and Tanya. "Well, looks like we're getting ready to pull out of here. Can I give you folks a ride to the hospital?"

"No, thanks. We're fine. I've got my vehicle parked a short ways from here and am perfectly capable of driving myself to the hospital."

"I'll be driving Wade to the hospital," Tanya corrected, her tone warning both men there would be no arguing the matter.

Wade rolled his eyes and grinned at Jansen over Tanya's head.

"Good luck, Scott," the detective offered with an amused smile as he held out his hand.

Wade clasped it tightly and pumped hard. "No hard feelings, Jansen?"

"Hell, no. Besides, it looks like you've got your work cut out for you as it is." He sauntered off, chuckling, leaving Wade and Tanya on their own together.

She eyed him uncertainly. "Do you really love me?" she asked in wonder, not quite daring to believe it. Then her face fell. "How can you?" she answered her own question, her voice laced with bitter regret. "After everything I did to you all those years, and what I said to you in the restaurant, I'm surprised you can even stand the sight of me."

He wrapped his good arm around her and offered one more reassuring hug. Releasing her, he placed a finger under her chin, tilting her head up gently to stare deeply into her eyes. "Yes, Tanya, I do love you. Have no doubts about that." A glint of amusement entered his eyes. "And as for how I could possibly love you? Well, it's true you're somewhat hotheaded, not to mention impulsive, stubborn as hell, and more than a little bossy, but you make life . . . interesting." He grinned down at her conspiratorially. "And I like that in a woman."

CPSIA information can be obtained at www.ICGtesting.com
Printed in the USA
LVOW06s1449070414

380663LV00001B/165/P